PRAISE FOR WAYNE CURTIS

Of all Canadian writers, Wayne Curtis is the one I keep coming back to. He is perhaps the greatest unsung talent in the country.

– David Adams Richards

A sensitive and insightful writer of the short story, Curtis' prose has a solid core and a rhythm that carries the reader along.

– Sinclair Ross

A seductive storyteller wholly immersed in the world he vividly creates, Curtis reveals himself to be a lyrical and sensuous stylist.

– *The Globe and Mail*

Curtis' prose is more true-to-life than most current short fiction.

– *Quill & Quire*

The prose of Wayne Curtis is beautiful to read, for no detail escapes his discerning eye.

– *Books in Canada*

Curtis has an eye for the telling detail, giving us the most information about a character in the fewest possible words.

– *New Brunswick Reader*

The closeness to detail vibrates with an honesty which bears witness to lives lived humbly and poignantly. Wayne Curtis is a splendid writer.

– Alistair MacLeod

WINTER ROAD

By

Wayne Curtis

POTTERSFIELD PRESS
Lawrencetown Beach, Nova Scotia, Canada

Library and Archives Canada Cataloguing in Publication

Title: Winter road : (short stories) / by Wayne Curtis.

Names: Curtis, Wayne, 1943- author.

Identifiers: Canadiana (print) 20200172700 | Canadiana (ebook) 20200172735 | ISBN 9781989725078

(softcover) | ISBN 9781989725085 (HTML)

Classification: LCC PS8555.U844 W56 2020 | DDC C813/.54—dc23

Front cover credit: www.123rf.com

Cover design by Gail LeBlanc

Pottersfield Press gratefully acknowledges the financial support of the Government of Canada for our publishing activities. We also acknowledge the support of the Canada Council for the Arts and the Province of Nova Scotia which has assisted us to develop and promote our creative industries for the benefit of all Nova Scotians.

Pottersfield Press
248 Leslie Road
East Lawrencetown, Nova Scotia, Canada, B2Z 1T4
Website: www.PottersfieldPress.com
To order, phone 1-800-NIMBUS9 (1-800-646-2879) www.nimbus.ns.ca

Printed in Canada

Pottersfield Press is committed to preserving the environment and the appropriate harvesting of trees and has printed this book on Forest Stewardship Council® certified paper.

For Cynthia

Action is consolatory. It is the enemy of thought
and the friend of flattering illusions.

– Joseph Conrad
Nostromo (1904)

CONTENTS

CLASS OF '59

MANY OF MY FRIENDS FROM STANTON HIGH SCHOOL have died in acts of devilry. My brother Andrew, always a tyrant, was killed at the age of seventeen when he "wrote off" our father's car while speeding around Kelly's Turn on the lower end of Main Street. He had been drinking whisky and trying to impress his girl-friend, who survived the crash. Ronald Green's life was lost in a head-on collision in sight of the village. He was driving home from Kingston, having taken his girlfriend to college. George O'Brien and Beverly Black succumbed to poisonous fumes on a winter's night, having fallen asleep in a parked car with the engine run-ning. Lloyd Creamer was pronounced dead after rolling his 403 Series Indian motorcycle in front of the dance hall on Main Street. He was drinking alcohol and, with a ramp, was trying to jump over two oil drums. His would-be lover was looking on. Sonny Gray was done in by mobsters in Montreal, having gotten mixed up in the selling of narcotics. Henry Kenny was sentenced to life in prison af-ter shooting a taxi driver in Bradford. They had squabbled over the price of a bootleg bottle of rum. These schoolmates rest, forever young, in our village churchyards. All were daring teenagers – some of whom, for a time, I tried to emulate – looking for attention, try-ing to make a name. They are just a few of the sixty-five students who were in my graduation class of 1959.

While the Stanton of my youth was a repellent old place, some good things did happen here. Donnie King, who was our musical influence, played his guitar through life and made it to Nashville Tennessee's Ryman Auditorium where, it is said, he performed at the Grand Ole Opry. Later he was inducted into the Country Music Hall of Fame. Carroll Rose became a doctor and practised medicine in Toronto for thirty-five years. Jimmy Darren made it in the plastic industry in Chicago and got very rich. (He was my best friend in class and we have exchanged Christmas cards for the sixty-odd years since.) Morris Davidson got to be an engineer and a bridge builder in the Northwest Territories. Mary Macbeth went to Toronto where she was a successful lawyer and a stockbroker. It is said that Mary is a multi-millionaire. And there are some men and women who did well in politics and the construction industry here at home.

Of course, I had different priorities and other goals to achieve, and these were not money related. Having inherited my mother's house, I stayed in the village and, without shame, played the organ in St. Paul's Anglican Church. For a time, I dabbled in the arts, while keeping a day job as bookkeeper for an angler's club. And I worked at the mill for the last five years before it was shut down, losing three fingers to the big saw, which ended my music career. Yes, I lived on the cutting edge and the sawmill kept a part of me when it closed. I remember coming home from work, coughing up phlegm and with sawdust in my hair. I was glad to have the inside work, a little security around home. But the men broke the union; that eventually broke the mill, which eventually broke the village. To find work, many young people scattered to the oil fields of Alberta. There was nothing left to do here, even though it was, and still is, the most beautiful place on Earth.

At the time of my graduation, Stanton had a busy Main Street that was the centre of gravity for all of Falconer County. Along that stretch of road – the through-street of Old Highway Eight – there was an active dance hall (two dances a week), a pool hall, movie house, two diners, a dozen stores, a sawmill, a morgue, and seven or eight churches whose spires reached above the river elms. On Sunday mornings there was a chorus of chimes that sent nesting pigeons into flight, while beckoning us to our respective places of worship. We dressed in our best Levi's, sport shirts, and half-Wellington boots and reluctantly went there with our mothers and fathers to crowd into the family pew and await the benediction.

Through high school, to earn pocket money, I sold my grandmother's newly fried doughnuts, with hot coffee from a thermos bottle, to the workers at the mill. For a small sum, I also mowed lawns for the villagers so that on Saturday nights I could buy a Coke, an order of french fries, and a cigarette for the girls – in their pleated skirts, white bucks, and Marilyn Monroe hairstyles – who hung out at Tim's Diner. Most of the lads strolled up and down the sidewalk – catching the glare of black and white televisions from living-room windows, *I Love Lucy, Our Miss Brooks* – before going into the restaurant where everyone gathered in the back room to play the jukebox and jive. It was that time in our lives when our whole future depended upon a dance with a certain young woman. Once, after an evening at the diner, Mary Macbeth took me to her house on Campbell Street and tried to teach me how to jive to Buddy Holly songs being spun on her portable record player. She said, "Dale, you are a nice guy but you will never be a dancer." As a jive meant more to me than just a "dance" and a good dancer was considered to have class, I was devastated. Because I knew that girls loved the guys who could boogie.

I can remember sitting at my desk in 12B and looking out the window at the distant sawmill. Men dressed in raincoats and sou'westers were using picks to drag the logs out of the millpond and put them on a conveyer that took them up to the screaming saws. A hedge of pine trees, tossed about by the April winds, screened the turbulent river below the dam, while a centuries-old horse hauled bark and slabs in a Red River cart to a furnace with its tall brick chimney that my grandfather had helped to build when he was a teenager. In the cold spring rain, the village looked shabby, the weather-beaten sheds having been painted black from the dampness. In the well-lighted classroom, I tried to keep alive the music from the previous Saturday night: Bobby Helms, "You Are My Special Angel" and Sonny James, "Young Love." They carried in their melodies my choice few friends, especially Mary, whose desk was across the room from mine and whose presence invoked my silent daydreams. Of course, with my bashfulness, these inward moments remained unspoken, except in the physical sense when I hugged her briefly on the dance floor. She always stressed that the alternative to schoolwork was the mill. "So pay attention to the teacher, and not to me!"

Because of pneumonia in the spring of '58, I missed two weeks at school and this brought with it a feeling of guilt and despair. At home alone, I had the suspicion that events outside the classroom, where I struggled with math, would not enhance my intelligence or my chances with Mary, and because of idleness I was losing ground. I had heard it said that women cannot love someone who is less intelligent than themselves. So in the diner I tried to mix with the guys I thought would impress her. But she was not to be moved and kept her feelings covered, like a deck of cards in its box, until I wondered if my love for her was more about my being lonely than the woman with the moving brown eyes and cute giggle. Well, at first I just loved her – the way it is with teens – and then I began to admire and respect her too.

For sure Mary was a great influence. She was level-headed, and had no time for frivolity. In addition, anything that you whispered to her was kept in confidence, which I considered a virtue among high school girls. Once she helped me write an essay. "You have to make each sentence unique within itself," she said. "Have it stand out, like a spotlight on the moment, a dog's bark among bird songs." I got a B-plus.

After school and on weekends Mary never stopped working. She did housework for her mother, who was employed at the diner, and she spent her Saturdays as a clerk at Kent's Furniture Store. She picked blueberries by the quart along the railway tracks, took in sewing jobs, and bought her own clothing. When in the fall of '58 her father had a stroke and was physically impaired, she asked

me if I would go with her to the woods, where near Dan's Brook in
the provincial park we cut a Christmas tree for her family. It was a
special day for me because, clandestinely, Mary and I were working
together in a common cause, with the same, though short-term,
goal.

But it was also fun to walk down the sidewalk with my
chums on summer Saturday nights when the setting sun was
in our faces and the heels of our polished leather boots made a
clicking sound on the warm cement. In reflection, our long, high-
stepping shadows stretched out behind us like so many ghosts, as
if nature had taken a lesson from art. Cars, with their white-wall
tires and yellow sponge dice that hung on rear-view mirrors, were
parked, bumper to bumper, along the street as the country people came to the village to shop or to dance. From the entryway of
the Public Dance Hall, I could hear the screech of the fiddle, the
howls of country singers – "So, darlin', save the last dance for me."
I could smell the cornmeal that had been sprinkled on the hardwood floor, the men's Old Spice aftershave. "I warm so easy, so
dance me loose," they shouted. They whooped and laughed.

Inside the hall, between sets, in their floral-print dresses,
open sandals, and arm bracelets, women sat on benches along the
walls, their legs crossed firmly at the knees. And there were pockets
of laughter among them. The men, some of whom were the fathers
of my classmates, wore white shirts with the sleeves rolled up, but
no neckties. They stood in groups, rolled cigarettes, passed around
a flask of Johnny Walker, and talked about how many cords of
pulpwood they had cut that week, how their fields of potatoes were
growing, or what kind of spring fishing they had had; all of which,
if done successfully, brought a lot of dignity to the country people. And the smell of raw whisky, tobacco smoke, sweat, and cheap
perfume mixed to give off a sour stench that I can still remember.
They were believers in Ford trucks, Ferguson tractors, Winchester
firearms, Shakespeare fishing tackle, Raleigh's Medicated Ointment,
and the Progressive Conservative Party of Canada. And they hated
the jerky music of Buddy Holly and Elvis Presley.

These men got together at dances, card parties, haying times, and pig killings. When, because of automation and big industry, that old way of life vanished – along with the bucksaw, axe, and the draft horse, and tourism became the driver of our river's economy – they were lost. They hated to change from the old ways where the accomplishments from hard work were such a big part of their everyday lives, their personal pride. They died from the loss of the life they knew, the changing times. The new service economy and the electronic age took something away from our river and our village. And this could never be replaced.

I was twelve years old in the summer of '53 when I saw four young men leave the dancehall and head to the bootlegger in Grand Rapids for more rum. They crowded into an old rod-knocking, blue Chevrolet that was missing on two cylinders, had smooth tires, one headlight, and Hollywood mufflers that spilled a gray smoke and a blatting noise into the street. They were laughing and whooping as they went over the hill to cross the river bridge. When the brakes gave out, down where the railway tracks were, the car swerved into the ditch and completely missed the bridge. They went over a thirty-foot embankment and into the river where water was up to their chins. But they managed to get out of the car, crawl up the riverbank, and stagger back to the dance. And I can remember seeing them standing in the entryway. Barefoot and soaked to the skin, they hugged one another and cried, the cheap violin bowing inside. It was the first time I ever saw a group of grown men cry. They were in shock and thankful to be alive.

Here, five hundred yards above the Grand Rapids, our river was dark and frothing, its banks fringed with pine trees, their extended branches making thin shadows on the water. The Grand Rapids is where this river roars so loud we could hear it from our bedrooms. The Chevy sat on the bottom of the river, surrounded by a million amber stones, and the water ran through its windows. An old straw hat drifted down with the currents. The wreck stayed there for three weeks and people from all over the county came to stand on the bridge and look down at the scene, wondering, I suppose, how the men survived such a fall, such deep water. "Well, if they had been sober they would all be dead," my uncle Joe said.

For a time after the accident, the Pentecostal minister held revival meetings in a big circus tent that was set up in the field between Campbell Street and Main Street. Through a loudspeaker, the women, in their ankle-length skirts and long hair, sang "Look to the lamb of God" while the cries of "Praise the Lord" and "Halleluiah" could be heard as far upriver as Falconer. For a prank, during the prayers, local teens threw green apples in under the skirts of the tent. Once, for excitement, some of the bigger lads simultaneously pulled the stakes that were holding up the canopy, so that when the minister was in his final plea, beseeching people to come to the altar to "be saved," the whole thing collapsed and everyone inside was screaming and looking for a way out. I guess you could say that the preacher brought down the roof that night. It was at this time that some of the men got religion, became "born-again Christians." And they preached the Gospel at the drop of a hat. But then after some weeks, they backslid, drank whisky again, and went back to the dances.

Saturday night was a time for all of us to look our best and have fun. We, the teenagers, were living not within ourselves, but rather the people we wanted to become – a kind of new reach dream place of rock 'n' roll music, electric guitars, Ivy League shirts, and Elvis haircuts, all of which were woven into the night's excitement. With a new age dream alive inside me, it was like I had already achieved my life's goals, but without the responsibilities of adulthood. My heart was light and happy, and life was bigger than all of outdoors. Yes, in the dream it was, but in real life there was always turbulence and uncertainties.

I can remember meeting Jimmy Darren on Main Street in that spring of '58. It was on the crowded sidewalk in front of Tim's Diner where from through the screened door we could hear the pulsating sounds of the jukebox: Guy Mitchell, "Singing the Blues." Jim's hair was slicked back with creams in the Elvis style and he was wearing a long-sleeve, Ivy League shirt, blue jeans, and the half-Wellington boots that had been made popular by James Dean in the movie *Rebel Without a Cause*. As we talked and smoked and looked over one another's hair – a calf lick in the front, duck tail in the back, and with long curly sideburns – I could smell his cologne. I could also scent the burnt onion flavours and tobacco smoke that drifted from the window fans of the restaurant. I could hear the tramping of feet and the high-pitched squeals of the young women, envision their laughing eyes under the peaks of baseball caps which were a fad at the time.

We went inside and stood at the back of the room and waited for a chance to dance. The women were dancing with one another and there were pockets of perfume drifting about the diner. Finally I jived with Mary. Heavy-footed, I was trying to spin her. When the waltz "Love Me Tender" was played, she broke away and went to stand with the girls. Later, Jimmy and I sat on stools at the L-shaped counter and ordered fish and chips and 7Up from Mary's mum, who was like a mother to us all. Along the bar, there were salt and pepper shakers, bottles of ketchup and vinegar, the soda fountain, and a punch board.

When it was dark outside, we walked up the street and stole into the old movie house to sit in the back row, eat popcorn, and watch the western picture shows of Randolph Scott and John Wayne. (Jim's father, John, was operating the projector and was blind to our charades.) Sometimes Mary came with us as she was a cousin to Jim. On other evenings, we went out to the railway station and watched the train come in. The Express, which was on its way from Bradford to Fredericton, stopped to drop off passengers who were coming from town. Once Mary climbed the ladder on a parked boxcar and ran on the roof, daring Jim and me to follow. And we dared one another to pee on the electric fence that surrounded the Connors' pasture. These simple things were our Saturday night rituals.

On Easter Sunday, Jimmy came into our church – he always sat in the balcony – wearing a Lone Ranger mask. Below the mask, he grinned and chewed gum as though in defiance of the priest.

When Father Bailey turned his back to prepare the host, Jim whistled at him in the way that one might whistle at a girl. It was then, red-faced, the priest stopped his homily and, pointing a finger at Jimmy, said, "Whoever that is wearing a mask and disrupting the service, get to hell out of this church!"

Everyone looked at Jim as he embarrassingly made his way outside.

The next Saturday evening as Jim and I walked down the street, past the United Church, we met Sonny Gray coming toward us. I always shivered when I met him, because I knew that when he had a drink he wanted to fight, and he fought dirty. It seemed like he carried a rebellious anger that came to the surface after he had just one sip. Of course he was always boozing on the weekends.

Through the week, in my father's closed-down store, we had been sparring with the boxing gloves and I knew he had some nifty moves. But this time he started taunting Jimmy, who was not a boxer but was solid as a rock. And when they got into a wrestling hold, Jim hit him hard in the stomach with his right fist – wham! – and knocked him backwards over the hood of the minister's car. It was the hardest punch I ever saw, a short right-cross that took the wind, and the fight, out of Sonny. I knew I would never mess with Jim. I kept on friendly terms with Sonny too, but I stayed away from him when he was drinking, because his eyes got wild and I never knew what he might do. Sonny never smiled, but was either dead serious or laughing. And from the grimace on his face it was hard to tell one of these emotions from the other. On the street in front of the restaurant, I had seen him and another classmate, fighting. They had knives flicking to cut holes in one another's jackets. Until the overweight village policeman – he had lost their respect – came and put them in the back of his patrol car and drove them home, warning them of the consequences if he caught them in the village again with knives and liquor.

Sonny was always getting expelled from school. He repeated the grades and eventually dropped out. I can remember seeing him in the first days of spring, as I walked back to school after being home for lunch. In shorts and bare-breasted, he was lying near the sluiceway on the old mill dam. Beside him on the planking stood a transistor radio – belting out the country music – a pack of Export A cigarettes, and a romance novel. And I often wondered if perhaps he was waiting for the muse to rise from music in the water to give him new ideas for devilry.

There was a gang of wild lads from lower Stanton, and a few dropouts from up Falconer way, who hung out on the mill bridge and sometimes started fights with passersby. Some of them carried knives and once, on Halloween night, they slashed the white-wall tires on a dozen cars that were parked along Main Street. Later, one of them told me that it was comical to stand in the dark and watch the barber, with a hand-pump, attempting to fill his inner tubes with air. He pumped and puffed for almost an hour before calling police. I remember Mounties coming to the school and questioning some of us about the crime, but no one told them anything. "I didn't see no one do nothin'," Sonny said. I believe that case is still open.

The barber operated a shop in the back of his house and none of us had an ounce of use for him. He refused to give us the Elvis haircut; instead he sniped off our sideburns, chopped and brushed our hair into a crew-cut style that had been popular five years earlier. When we complained, he said he had been instruct-ed by our parents to "snip it close." Well, he had asked for the tire trouble; that's what everyone in the school believed.

On a September night in '58 some of the lads from 12A killed and butchered a heifer that had been pastured in the Adams' field. (In the car lights they had been jacking deer and fired a rifle shot at two glaring green eyes.) The next morning – before Mr. Adams realized he was missing a young cow – they sold the meat, driving a half-ton truck from door to door through the vil-lage. Of course they were arrested by Mounties because of there having been so many witnesses. They had to pay Frank Adams for his loss. This inspired some of them to write a song that they set to the tune of "Mary of the Wild Moor":

Oh, how the old man must have felt,
When he went to the field the next morn.
There was a hide and a head but the heifer she was dead,
As the wind blew across the Adams' shore.

Sometimes Donnie King, Jimmy, and I would go to one of our parents' house to play music and sing. We all played guitars, some of which were electric. I can still hear the squealing feedback from the amplifiers and the vibration of the wah-wah pedals. We took part in the amateur shows that were held in the United Church Hall when the singing cowboys came to hold their concerts. We played the simple Ventures tunes like "Walk, Don't Run" and "Apache." Performing, we got into the shows for free.

On prom night, in the school auditorium, dressed in white sports coats and black trousers we drank pop from paper cups, smoked tobacco in the entryway, and danced, having gotten a date with a cousin. (Jimmy had gone to Bradford where, in Black's Clothing Store, he bought a new suit and charged it to John MacKann, the taxi driver in Stanton who was well-to-do.) Mary, who was voted to be "Queen of the Prom," invited a guy from Bradford to go with her, so I could not dance with her that night. She wore a flared hot-pink dress, matching high-heel shoes, and a white rose. Anyone could see that she had loads of class. After the dance, we drove our fathers' cars to the provincial picnic site on Dan's Brook where a wiener roast was happening. Some parked their vehicles in wood roads and wrestled with the girls to have sex. It was rumoured that two young women were raped by guys who were drinking alcohol. Another girl might have been assaulted had she not jumped from the car and run, in bare feet, through mud, back to the fire site. She slipped back into the group where everyone was singing to the music of Donnie's guitar. One of the women raped – she was from Cole's Siding – got pregnant and, fearing a scandal, married the guy who violated her. She still lives with him in that community where they have raised a large family. "Well, she must have had some feelings for the man," my mother said.

This was before the days when I owned a like-new '54 Chevy hard-top I had bought for three hundred dollars from a man in Bradford, my father having co-signed for the loan. It was a classic car and I drove it with pride.

In that Chevy, smoking cigarettes, I checked my hair in the rear-view mirror before driving to Mary's house to take her for a ride. She would leave her homework and come with me only once in a while. We motored through the village with the windows cranked down and the radio blasting the songs of The Big Bopper and Patsy Cline. When I tramped down the gas pedal and that 409 engine caught on fire, the big Chevrolet floated on air. And I honked my horn to make an echo as we drove through the barn-like covered bridges in Upper Stanton.

Once I took Mary to the drive-in theatre where we watched bits and pieces of *The Tall Men*, while steaming up the car windows. That night I wanted to tell her that I loved her, but thought better of it, because I could sense her feelings toward me were not that strong, and that she looked upon me simply as a friend and classmate, and that I was really getting too serious. Soon she wanted to leave the theatre as she had work to do at home. Yes, even her indifference was genuine. Still, I carried Mary's love inside me like a virus. And I wondered if time would heal all the torture I felt because of her indifference toward me. (She is with me even now as I write this.) I know for a fact that we go on loving those whom we cannot fully possess. Or maybe it simply becomes a habit. And many times, through the years, the would-be affair brought me feelings of shame and self-pity. Yet I was comforted by the memory of her in my arms, be it ever so briefly.

I eventually wrote off the Chevy – and was almost killed – when, trying to pass a snowplow on a blind hill, I had a head-on collision with a pickup truck. Thank God that Mary was not in the car. I was charged with "dangerous driving" and lost my driver's licence for five years, which extended well beyond my final days of high school.

I remember cramming for my final exams, stealing a look at Mary's answers, and the relief I felt after the tests had been passed in and were marked by the teachers. When I finally got my report card and knew I did not have to repeat grade twelve, I felt a great sense of freedom. Summer holidays were in sight.

Of graduation day I can recall the march being played on the school piano, my mother's tears. I remember walking across the blue-curtained stage for the handshake and ribbon-tied diploma, the beautiful voice of Angela White singing, "The One Rose (That's Left in My Heart)" and afterwards streaming into the parking lot to be embraced by parents, posing for a photograph, and then a fast drive with classmates to Dan's Brook for an all-night barbecue. During the night some of the guys set fire to the wooden bridge that crossed over the stream and this brought firefighters and police. It is another case that is still open.

It was right after graduation that most of the class left Stanton and moved on to bigger and better things, in cities from coast to coast and abroad. After Mary and Jimmy left, the village was like a wasteland, without a spirit or a cause. And when the maple trees caught on fire with reds and yellows, and were then stripped bare by the cold winds of November, I shivered as I walked alone between the diners. There seemed to be so many long autumn and winter evenings to endure without the ones that mattered. "People make the place," my mother used to say when she spoke about how things used to be when she was a girl at home in Grand Rapids. But I knew that Mary would always be with me spiritually, as so much of our relationship was planted deep in my psyche. In fact, she had become a state of mind, one that brought me more suffering than pleasure. I also knew that forgetting her, if I could, would yield me some peace, if only in the minor key. Because the subtle inward metaphors – as I looked deep inside myself – told me it was hopeless and that she would never let something as fleeting as *love* get in the way of her ambitions to achieve great things. How I longed for her in those days after she went away.

Gone too now is the movie house, the pool hall, the diners, dry goods stores, sawmill, morgue, and the white clapboard Stanton High School. The false-fronted buildings that stand along Main Street – the vacant dance hall, train station, and some closed-down stores – are ghostly and await the wrecking ball. Only a few can remember when these structures had a purpose. But the ghosts in those old buildings still speak to me. Walking down that lonely sidewalk, if I listen carefully, I can hear the pounding of the jukebox in the back of Tim's Diner, the jingle of cash registers behind the store facades, the whisper of voices in commerce, the laughter from the open doors of the dancehall. And I still see as young the people I had known young. It is hard for me to remember when that old day ended, and my adult life began.

In their stead are the new steel and glass Stanton Village Hall, the brick elementary and high school, fire station, ambulance headquarters, an ultra-modern medical centre, seniors' complexes, and a giant supermarket that is built from stone. These buildings now serve the more sprawling, more electronic service community with the current-day necessities; our newspapers come online, and home delivery is from Amazon. Everyone is driving a new car, has a cell phone, a boat, and a wilderness cabin in which to retreat. The streets and the back lanes of the village have lost their social significance and are nothing more than a means in which to get around.

But I can recall as a small boy going into Gorman's Department Store, then such an important establishment in our village. That business, where many of our mothers worked, was a big part of our culture, like the music we played; like our fistfights against the world; like the hedges of hawthorn in our backyards, the birds and bees of childhood. I went upstairs, to where I did my Christmas shopping with six dollars. For my grandmother I bought a bottle of Bufferin (for timely pain relief), a pair of cotton work-gloves (by Stanfield's) for Father, a pack of fifty-two playing cards (made in Canada by Bicycle) for my brother Alex, and for Mum, a box of Oxydol Laundry Detergent (it eliminates all stains) by the makers of Proctor and Gamble. I had enough money left to buy a pack of Sportsman Cigarettes (by the makers of Black Cat – *The world lights up with a Sportsman*) that cost forty-four cents.

After sixty years had passed, and the cold rains of autumn were in the air, over the west end of Main Street hung a blue and yellow banner welcoming *The Class of '59*. In the new school auditorium at the "Meet and Greet" I found some of my classmates – gray-haired and lame, once able souls, now leaning on canes. Some were in wheelchairs. My friends from the old days – I could not remember their names – looked like bad reproductions of old portraits or waxed figures that had been stood too close to open flames and had melted. Others were overdecorated and artificial, like the plastic flowers we see in graveyards. Wearing hearing aids and bifocals I read nametags before shaking hands with men and women who did not remember me. Of course none of these people were looking for recognition, as the old home crowd, the few that remained, and our little social worlds, meant nothing to anyone but ourselves. Jimmy and his wife Linda had come from Chicago. Like old times, we sat on tin chairs at a paper-covered steel table and drank Cokes from Styrofoam cups. And our teacher, a well-aged Sarah Donelly, once a master of the piano, stumbled over the keys, as those who were able stood to sing our school song, "Stand Up and Shout for Old Stanton High." More moving still was when we all held hands and the aged Glee Club made an attempt to render "Auld Lang Syne."

Then Donnie King's Reunion band played "True Love Ways," "Love me Tender," "Johnny B. Goode," "Runaway," and "Breaking Up is Hard to Do."

Indeed, the old music in the jukebox had started up all over again. The songs carried in their lyrics a time when our car radios kept alive our passions through the long school week between dates. (They bring them to life even now.) Quite a few people were even dancing.

Across the room I could see Mary Macbeth, more radiant than a morning in June and with the same dreamy smile we see in portraits. Having all the freshness of charm and youth, she appeared, in fact, as proper as the woman I carried inside myself, the telling nature of nostalgia not being undone by reality. (Along the way, I had been attracted to her features in other women, some of whom were accessible. So the ultimate reality was that through time I had suffered the loss of more than one Mary Macbeth. There had been a woman with the same nose in Sussex, another with Mary's brown eyes in St. Andrews by-the-Sea, another with her dimpled smile and ultra white teeth in Bathurst. These women had run in my mind for a time in parallel with Mary, so that now suddenly there was a rebirth of glad moments from them all.)

But after so many years of absence, it was great to watch Mary jive with her husband, who seemed insecure and overprotective. (I thought, jealousy is a disease of the flesh and ours was a Platonic, mind relationship.) Indeed, she was no less beautiful – although at this point her identity was more important to me than her beauty – and I could hear the same cute giggles, see her attempt to swing the impossible dancer. Mary caught my glance, my nod, which of course was inviting, always inviting. And how I would have liked to have danced with her. She looked at him, and then at me, with a show of gentleness that was more telling than words. Better not, was her message, but with a politeness that displayed a refined and dignified lady. And I knew that the words I whispered in her ear so long before, the old confidences, were never broken. Her whole demeanour belonged to yesterday. It offered a message of condolence, the old romantic notions having resurfaced for a quick moment. But just as quickly were set free, as they had been years before when she left the village.

I realized that there had been many experiences Mary had that I had not, and that our time apart, and philosophic growth, had only served to further distance ourselves from one another, as she was by this time a world traveller, her reflections, however remote to me, being from a higher viewpoint. And I felt that the little moments – so strong in my mind – from being with her would have been overshadowed by the bigger things in her life, since she went away. Nevertheless, my feelings were proof to me

that, like a wild goose or a Canada jay, people nurture one principal love through life, whether that love is reciprocated or not. And
I knew that to dance with a lesser woman would only make more
cruel that of my first love's indifference. So I took my place in the
shadows and watched. It was an old habit that brought me some
peace of mind, if not peace of heart. For sure, I had always been in
a cloud when it came to Mary.

It was a time when words would have failed me, as before,
so the feelings remained locked in, as before. They are locked in
even now, especially now. There had never been adequate language
– even during school days – that would describe the feelings I nurtured for Mary. And the pleasure of my having been with her, even
briefly, remains unspoken and has been kept strong, perhaps because of her absence. I had made a point to keep it strong, keep
her in a special place, the old wound having long scarred over.
And I knew that to open it again would only mean more anxious
doubts. In retrospect, I suppose that Mary had aged too, and listening to her voice – which was the same – I was seeing her through
the lens of an eighteen-year-old lover. As Marcel Proust put it,
"There must be something inaccessible in what we love, something to pursue; we love only what we do not possess." Of course
I did not possess Mary Macbeth, not for an evening. I lived a soli-
tary life, exploiting the seductiveness of memory, coloured in my
favour by nostalgia. But I took some pride in the fact that my feelings were not innocent, but mature, not provincial, but universal.
I had been waiting to dance with Mary for sixty years, while Donnie's Reunion Band played the Ricky Nelson song "There's a Place
Called Lonesome Town."

We'll always have Stanton, I thought.

"Where is the old village, the railway tracks, the sawmill, the
old gang? Where have the years gone?" Jimmy wanted to know.
"The place appears so small, so dull and lifeless."

"Everything looks the same to me," I told him. "Like old
times, everyone is here who matters."

When I looked across the room again, Mary was gone.

AWAY, BACK EAST

THEY DROVE FROM TORONTO TO MONTREAL ON Highway 401 and were taking the old Number Two East, cruising past Quebec City and Levis and heading on down the St. Lawrence River Valley. They found the air was getting fresher with each mile travelled.

"This is the most beautiful country I ever saw," Pam said. She was looking in all directions as though afraid she would miss something. They passed a grindstone in someone's dooryard, a winnowing machine beside a garden wall: personal touches of the woods and farm that were a part of the culture, and which inspired Mark to boast, as a contemporary, to their purpose. But he knew that Pam had no idea what these vestiges stood for and the moments of reflection, triggered by the scenery, did not exist for her.

But for Mark, who had grown up in this end of the country, the farm implements were like phrases in a symphony of classical music. They made up the "whole" when it came to looking at a landscape that brought back so many emotions. The inventiveness of memory carried him along through the wooded stretches between farms. And at the end of lanes the tree-shaded farmhouses (that to him were the only kind of house worth looking at) served to further embody the rugged and rustic soul. And he felt that he had never completely outgrown that age of innocence, and probably never would.

But he knew that moving back home was something he had to do. While he figured the landscape would serve as a reminder of old times, even hardship, he knew he wanted to be back with all the recollections that memory could bring. And he thought, The life has stayed with me in spirit, long after it had left me in fact. He also knew this spirit could never be broken. People are like homing birds or fish, he thought.

He looked at Pam, who sat smoking a cigarette. And while he loved her and would never let her go, he felt he could cover his inner emotions, his love for the land, the old ways, keep it concealed at the bottom of his heart. (She had warned him about living in the past and that it was a dangerous precedent.) He knew there was a great spirit in the woods and fields, places to heal from the tedious routine and the hard knocks that had depressed him in the unionized factories and the disciplined city life as well. He thought of the words of Proust: "We are all obliged, if we are to make reality durable, to house a few little follies within ourselves."

"So what are ya thinkin? You seem to be in that dark zone again."

"No no, I'm healing now; just reading the scenery. I spent my boyhood and adolescence in this end of the country." Mark kept his eyes on the highway, one hand on the steering wheel.

"How much further to the old place?"

"It's a good two hundred miles or more."

"Wow. Look at that river!" She pointed. "It's so pink in the sunset."

The orange-crayoned highway led them through grassy meadows where a stone cathedral, its silver spire with the neon cross, gleamed in the fading light. Between the poles, the power lines flashed red, like so many sizzling cat's cradles, the insulators green ice-cream scoops on the double-cross arms. Along the shore, yellow fishing shanties stood on stilts while boats, buttoned down with tarpaulins that looked like women's bonnets, lay moored in red grass. Mark glanced into the rear-view mirror to see once more the church, with its flaming cross, that stood against the sunset as it changed its position, and indeed its spirit, in sequence to the moving car. It seemed to say, "Welcome back to God's country, old friend."

"You'll like my folks and they'll like you too," Mark said.

"I hope so. But don't you get depressed again and become anti-social like you did in Ontario."

"I won't. That was a city thing. I'm at home in this country and will think and say what I want and when I want to, and in my own words too." Mark thought, For once I have someone who thinks she understands where I come from and where I am heading. "Pam, I love you," he said, as if he felt she could read his thoughts and needed reassurance just then.

"I love you too." She squeezed his right arm.

"You'll become a part of this landscape too," he said, as though to test her conviction to his cause.

"You make me feel like a somebody, though you're a bit in the dark zone since you started the literature courses at Brock."

"Classic poetry is a whole new world for me."

Mark thought of his old home in Falconer – a train-stop more than a place, a few houses surrounded by woods, big fields, and the home river, Miramichi. It was six miles upriver from Stanton, seventeen from Blueberry Ridge, and thirty-three from the old town of Bradford, which is on the Bay. For a moment he could see his young self back home, taking care of farm animals, splitting firewood, carrying water from the spring. There were no fraternity sweaters, no baseball uniforms, no golf or music lessons, no yoga classes, just hard work: the chopping of stove wood, weeding of vegetable gardens after long days in the woods with Papa-Jo. No, there was only wrangling, with a shout now and then to "work harder, boys, get the lead out of your arses" and maybe a western picture show on Saturday nights, a bit of tobacco to smoke as they walked along the gravel road to Stanton. The old place still came to him in the scent of a log fire, the music of flies, reminders of a time in his life when he was as transparent as a bee's wing, lacked confidence and direction. And there had been his grade eight teacher who told him to "Get a trade, take a barbering course." He had tried to turn these things into something positive since leaving, but had run into road blocks in Ontario as well. Until he realized that real success was important only if his own people could watch him make it happen. And he knew that coming back was something he had to do.

"When you get to see it you'll understand."

"If it is what you say it is."

"It's all of that and more."

In a crib in the back seat, Nathaniel slept. He had been born the previous winter, just four months after the wedding, a quiet kid to a working mum and dad in a town rich in the arts, history, and architecture. But while Pam and Mark had good-paying jobs in factories, a good car, a decent apartment, and Mark had a golf membership at the Niagara Golf Club, he yearned to get back east because the Ontario mentality – the running and falling to save for a down payment on a bungalow, the bullying of big union politics, the rat-race among so many people whom he felt were without souls – depressed him.

It was after ten p.m. when they arrived in Falconer. Turning in the gravel lane at the old place, Mark honked the horn and could see his family, in bare feet, clamouring out into the dooryard to greet them. They had been getting ready for bed, which embarrassed Mark. Having been used to doing night shift at the factory and going to clubs, he seldom got to sleep before three a.m., especially on weekends, although this had changed since meeting Pam. He knew it would take a while to adjust back into the old way, reacquaint with the spirit and soul of a family not seen in over five years. But he felt that he could find his old self here, start over again. And he wanted to make Pam feel comfortable among them. He had almost forgotten the family nicknames, that homely but loving touch of kinfolk: Papa-Jo (Joseph), Mama-Jo (Dorothy), Toots (Jack), Sacker (Randy), Caley (Colleen), and his own, Mickey, a handle they had hung on him when he was a kid because he was slow-growing and short. And he was also ashamed because the old place looked small and shabby, the orange grass in the dooryard in need of mowing. But on the front lawn, the old elm tree flapped its leaves as if in applause – like it was drumming up a thunderstorm – while Caley carried the sleeping child into the house.

Mark hugged his mother, such a pretty woman in her youth, and could feel her emotions, her sensitivity. Squinting behind wire-framed glasses, and blinking to hide a tear, her tired face was pale, her hair having gone white, braided at the sides, doll-like – something she always did for a special occasion – her striking blue eyes appearing gray in this light. There were no words. But he could hear her deep sighs, like the whisper of trees in river winds. And he knew this was a big day in her life. He remembered her many long letters of encouragement while he was away. "Try to stay the course," she had written. "You have potential and there is nothing to do back here but to grow old."

After they had embraced and wiped their tears, Mark asked "Where's Papa-Jo?"

"He's there in the house." Sacker motioned toward the front room.

Mark hurried past his brother, through the screen door and into the parlour where his father sat sleeping with a hand on each arm of an easy chair. He was not much more than a skeleton, his face drawn, his plaid shirt oversized, a pack of tobacco in his shirt pocket. Mark awakened him and the old man stood up, as if in a daze. He staggered and, leaning one leg against the chair for support, embraced his son. Papa-Jo trembled and wept openly, grasping a big red handkerchief from his pocket.

Mark could not put two words together. "Five . . . years . . . too . . . long . . . too . . . long."

"Too long, son . . . too long." The old man's cracked voice came in spurts and there was a whistle in his breathing.

"You . . . look . . . great!" The old place . . . looks . . . great!

"Why did ya . . .? Why did ya go away like that and stay so long, Mickey?" Papa-Jo was crying openly now, his shoulders heaving as he flag-tailed the handkerchief.

Mark clung to his father's arms that appeared frail under the shirt. And the old family portraits in their gilded frames stared down on them.

To help cover the moment, Caley, laughing and crying, joined the hug with her mother, until the whole family had gathered in a group hug, Pam among them.

When the car was unloaded, Mark was asked by Sacker (who was now almost thirty-five) about the golf clubs in the trunk. Explaining the reason for their different lengths, head sizes, and lofts, Mark demonstrated his swing in the beams of the car lights. He put a tee into the ground and, using the longest shaft, drove a golf ball a hundred and fifty yards toward the river.

"Wow! Did yuz see that?" Sacker shouted.

"I took lessons. I was club champion in B Division."

"Mickey, I have a day's trout fishing planned for us," Sacker said. "Back the brook."

"Great!"

"On Wednesday I'd like all of us to go to Bradford in your car," Toots put in. "Ontario licence plates. Maybe if it ain't raining we can put the top down?"

"Sure."

Resting an arm on the shoulder of his older brother, Mark could smell the sweat and tobacco smoke that was steeped into his clothes, his bachelor-uncle breath. For an instant he felt a touch of sadness because his brothers had not been away, and would never go away, at least not to stay, as he himself had not been able to do in the big part of Canada without long periods of melancholy. It was like they looked upon him as being, not ambitious, but privileged. And they looked upon Pam as some kind of city royalty, even though she had been hard-born and raised in Dain City, the outskirts of Port Colborne, and had also quit school in grade eight to work as a papermaker.

Papa-Jo, who was rolling and smoking cigarettes, said, "Mickey, thank you for sending a little money home to help with the well-diggers. We have running water and a bathroom, so you don't have to show your woman the smelly old backhouse." He took his son by the arm and walked with him into the kitchen, which to Mark also appeared small and shabby. "You won't find any half-pails of water on the washstand, no slop-buckets to be emptied. And look! We have an electric stove so you got no wood-boxes to fill."

Laughter.

"I hear the chicken coop and pigsty are gone too?"

"Yes, and you won't have to spend any of your vacation hauling in hay."

"Thank God," Mark said, recalling the sneezing fits that came from his hay fever.

Mark looked at his mother, now sitting near the sink, in her flowered housedress and slanted shoes, and remembered her, much younger, on her knees with a scrub brush, washing the floor of that kitchen, hacking away the black patches of chewing gum that were ground into the pine boards. She would scrub that floor until it was the colour of honey. That was how Mama-Jo worked and that was how she prayed, on her scarred knees. She had endured the labour with a Christian fortitude. Now, Mark could see in her a feeling of nervous energy, blushing like she felt bashful in the presence of this young city woman. He could detect her embarrassment, even shame, at what little she had. He knew that this old farmhouse, with its wainscot kitchen, wallpapered rooms, and a hundred doilies, was her world, except maybe when she went to church or to a prayer meeting. This confinement might have been said of Papa-Jo too, although he had the woods, fields, and river in which to ramble, the routine that came with each, to keep his mind nourished. But Mark knew that neither of them would ever leave this place.

"People don't need much when they have each other," Papa-Jo said, looking down at the floor and shaking his head. He had met Mama-Jo in the summer of '36 at a basket social up at The Forks, had married her that fall when he was seventeen and she was sixteen. "I went up to The Forks to spoon," he joked.

"Joe, don't tell that old stuff. Can I get yuz a cup a tea?" Mama-Jo said, nodding toward the stove.

"No thanks," Mark said, adding, "Mama-Jo, what a nice dress you're wearing."

"It's an old thing I had on all day." Her face reddened and she faked a smile and looked down to smooth out wrinkles in the skirt, pulling back her bunioned feet with bent knees. This made Mark feel guilty because he was driving a good car, had a golf membership and nice clothes, all of which he could have done without to send more money home, make life a bit easier for the most honest and the hard-working woman in Canada.

For a split second he remembered her attending to his asthma when he was a child, feeding him sugared tea and reading his awkward little poems to relatives on Sundays. She lived without many of the finer things and it grieved him to see that she was living without them even now, and so did not miss them. She had a tendency to see the worst side of things – which were in fact mostly true – with all its sad country inclinations, he thought. And while she was a good reader, he knew she always felt threatened by educated people. He figured that of the two women, his mother deserved the moral high ground, although Pam had travelled a hard road too, the early parts of which she despaired of remembering. We should never apologize for what we have or don't have, he reasoned. None of us in either family ever got a break.

"She gets high-toned when she puts on that dress," Papa-Jo said and winked at Pam, who was by now calling everyone by their nickname, even the old people.

Sitting in work clothes and with spruce pitch under his fingernails, it was obvious that Papa-Jo still worked the long days in the heat, fighting mosquitos as he cut pulpwood for ten dollars a cord and came home for supper, after which he worked until dark around the barns and gardens. That was how it used to be for them all. That was how it would always be for him. Mark could see his father's frail arms under the loose shirt, arms that had picked him up when he was a boy, arms that poled the big plank boats against the water's flow on the log drives, arms that had buck-sawed ten thousand cord of pulpwood. These were also the arms that had braced into the shearing earth, against the tug and toss of the plow handles, as he stumbled to keep pace with the fast-walking team, one crumbling furrow at a time, until the three-acre oat field was turned upside down and it was time to come into the house at suppertime. It had been dinner at noon and supper after dark. Mark had never seen his father in shorts or sandals and while his hair was now white as cotton, his face wrinkled and bronzed, below his shirt collar, his skin was pale and smooth as a china doll. As was his mother's. Sacker was the only one with a suntan.

The wooden telephone on the wall rang, in two short spurts. Pam nodded to Caley and then toward the phone. "It's not our ring," Caley said. "It also jingles when lightning comes in on the wires."

Later Mark watched his mother climb the stairs, clinging to the banister, labouring in her bare feet, to show Mark and Pam to his former bedroom. "I almost think we overdid it for one day," she said. "So much excitement around the old place, I hope nothing bad happens because of it." He felt a touch of embarrassment for taking Pam – though they were married – to his old bed, his mother watching and reading his thoughts. She would remember the devastation, the eagerness to succeed that Mark had felt before he went away. It was almost spooky how Mama-Jo could read his feelings. She spoke to Pam, who was standing with the baby on her hip, her blonde hair stringing down her shoulders, feet in loose, high-heeled shoes. "Mark will always be that little boy with the asthma, but with a fire in his belly."

"Yes, on fire for sure!"

"Nervous asthma conditions lose their force as one grows older," Mark said, remembering how disagreeable he had been through those illnesses.

And now there was Nathaniel to consider. He was put to bed in the old homemade cradle, now painted green. Mark could remember saying his prayers with his mother before going to sleep in that cradle. There had been ant holes in the rough, whitewashed boards. The same old flower-scrolled paper, wrinkled in the corners, was on the walls. The same old bureau with no handles on the drawers, the school picture of Megan Freeman, stuffed into the tilted mirror's frame, and a stack of western comic books. Standing in the corner was his old thirty-thirty rifle.

"Your gun is still there where you left it," Mama-Jo said. "I didn't let no one touch it."

At the foot of the bed was the worn-out rocking chair from Mark's childhood. For a moment he remembered Mama-Jo rocking him in that chair, the hand-hewn rocker that Papa-Jo had made, causing the chair to squeak as it walked across the floor, so that it would have to be picked up and set back in the centre of the room. Mama-Jo could do this without breaking the rhythm.

"I can see the lifestyle is rugged, but I like the people," Pam said when Mama-Jo had gone and they were under the covers. Mark lay sleepless in the now unfamiliar bed, which had a squeaky groove in the slat-spring centre.

"That picture on the bureau, who is she?"

"She was a school friend who grew up across the river. We used to fish trout together." For an instant Mark could see her, standing on the shore, holding the long juniper pole under one arm while he baited her hook with an angle worm. "She died when she fell from a hay loft onto the barn floor while feeding her father's horses," Mark said. "I was in grade seven and she was in grade eight when it happened." Pam has no idea how rugged this country can be, he thought. Rural children have no advantages. Even the good times are cut short by having to work long hours and in dangerous places, just to survive. And socially, these things have their effect on people too. I can see that now.

In the melancholy August morning, there was a hint of autumn in the air, the sun yellowing, a breeze crisp at the window. Papa-Jo lit a small fire in the parlour stove. This was something he had done in the old days when Mark was still in school – because his son had suffered from asthma – to take the dampness out of the upstairs bedrooms. Back then, because of the medications Mark had gotten from Dr. Duffy, when he looked out the window, instead of seeing the gables of the barn, he saw an artist's sketch of the gables of the barn, faded in weak pastel colours, at a slant against the foggy morning light, as in an Eliot poem, the sleepless night and the drugs having distorted the facts to give the scene more than one dimension. Until Dr. Duffy changed the medication, saying the pills were hard on his heart.

Now the smell of the burning wood, an aroma that Mark had forgotten because of his years away, took him back to those early autumns of his boyhood, when he was well and went to a woods camp with his father to look for deer, an old way of life that had been long since outgrown. He got out of bed and went to the window to see if the landscape had any of the same characteristics as of old – the weathered barns, the hayfields, which now seemed so much smaller and having gone fallow. Some houseflies buzzed between the screen and the window glass, sounding like a far-off chainsaw, "the sign of a storm," his father used to say. He could picture Papa-Jo in a mackinaw coat, felt hat, and with a galvanized pail of milk in each hand, as he walked toward the summer kitchen where he would do the cream separating. He could picture the sweet-smelling hay ricks, the swallows that flitted about the eaves of the barn.

And he thought, Oh, what I'd give to walk again in those fields after the hay was cut, where the stubble pinched my toes and the beckoning cherry trees offered up their low-hanging treats. Mark could smell the burnt-toast flavours that were coming from the kitchen. And he knew that he would be lying if he said that he was not a tad lonesome for those old days: the taste of buckwheat pancakes from the skillet, the smell of fresh pork strips sizzling on the woodstove, baked beans from the oven, fried eggs, home-fried potatoes, and the brew of bulk tea.

He could recall the story his mother had told him about the day he was born. It was in February of '44. Back then, before the new road was built ('48), they had lived a half-mile off the highway, through a pine woods and blustery fields. Dr. Hamilton arrived at noon from Stanton with Johnny Layton driving his horse and sleigh. Along with midwife Donna Gray, a neighbour from the next farm, they waited, until the baby arrived at four p.m. (Toots had been born in the Bradford hospital, also in February, five years earlier; Papa-Jo's brother, Uncle Jack, had driven Mama-Jo to the train station on the portage sled with the horse trotting through knee-deep snow. Because of complications she had been confined there for five weeks before coming home on the train, the baby in her arms. Sacker and Caley came later and without complications.) For a moment Mark thought of these wonderful people, long dead, but whose images appeared to him like characters out of an old Russian novel.

He remembered how welcoming his mother had been to strangers who happened to drop by, selling Raleigh's patent medicine, Fuller Brush, easy-to-read picture Bibles, or even young pigs. Sometimes they were just hobos who had nothing to sell. She always gave them a hot meal and sometimes asked them to stay the night. These people slept on the old cretonne folding bed. Once a blind man came to tune the piano and stayed three days. He brought the piano up to standard pitch and then concert pitch after which he rebuilt the old pump organ, parlour mice having eaten off the reeds. Mama-Jo was that kind of woman who would never let anyone go hungry or without a place to sleep. These things came to Mark now as he stood by the window, looking over the property.

That day the family went for a ride into Bradford, with Toots driving Mark's car at a funeral speed, steady but not fast. Mama-Jo and Papa-Jo sat in the back seat with Caley between them. And shadows of the car, dome-shaped, followed them along in the littered ditches. They waved to people they did not even know, much in the way that King George VI and Queen Elizabeth had done along this same road in 1939. And for that special moment, Mark could tell they felt just as important. He was proud that he was able to give his parents this special day, something they would talk about to neighbours for years after. Nearing the railway, Toots slowed the car to look for a train, even though the trains were no longer running.

Tall burdocks and overripe nettles stood along the shoulders of the highway, with purple sage, glittering with raindrops, among the birch trees along the fern-covered slopes. Ah, home, Mark thought. Birches are closer to the heart because they are a northern tree, so white and beautiful. There had been no birch trees in Niagara-on-the-Lake. The car splashed into the little pockets of brown water that stood on the road from the morning's shower, a black cloud having blown down the river, both indications of broken weather to follow. After the thunderstorm the weather was sunny but cool, and on the breeze the smell of poplar woodsmoke from chimneys of summer kitchens.

They passed the half-grown-up fields of the old McKinnon place, the gray barn standing, the house's stone foundation surrounded with lilac and apple trees. Mark could remember when the fields were cultivated and the big, brick-sided house, with its veranda facing the river, was a place to go and play music with the McKinnon boys. They had played music secretly, behind the barn, as old man McKinnon was a Baptist and would not let them play anything in the house but hymns. But all gone now. And he wondered what would become of his own old home property after Mama-Jo and Papa-Jo were gone. Would it fall into the hands of Sacker, the youngest son, or would it go to the government for taxes, like the McKinnon place? They drove through the breezy afternoon – the air keen after the shower – stopping for ice cream at a roadside stand. And then they went back home to kick off their shoes and have a cup of tea.

On Labour Day, Caley, overweight and chain-smoking, took Pam in the canoe where they drifted idly through the cool holiday afternoon. When Pam cast a dry-fly into the mouth of MacCord Brook and salmon broke water and grabbed it, she screeched and danced. Caley showed her how to play out the fish and not try to crank it in when it was too green for scooping.

"The Atlantic salmon is the highest jumper," she told Pam. "And we are on the best of all salmon rivers."

For a short while when the salmon was running away from the boat, it was a fifteen pounder, but as it tired and came near them, it was a six pounder again. The women stayed on the river until the water turned purple in the post-sunset, the bank trees darkened into the earth, and a premature harvest moon appeared on the treetops. Mark and Papa-Jo went to look for them and brought them back for supper, late though it was. "I think my stomach has collapsed I am so hungry," Pam said. She had been cupping her palms and drinking river water.

In the morning, with Toots driving Mark's car, the men went to the Falconer Fair where there was a horse-hauling contest. Mark stayed home from this, because of his allergies to horses. Instead, he and his mother went in Sacker's truck to visit the churchyards. Having planned on hauling the summer's cuttings of pulpwood to the boxcars, Sacker had welded a trailing-axle onto the back frame of the old Dodge half-ton. Mark found that these extra wheels – with snow tires and the tall hardwood stakes on its flatbed – made the vehicle hard to steer. He also found a half-flask of rum in the glove compartment. But he said nothing. Still, he knew that his mother would no longer go to church in that truck; rather she had asked Toots to drive her there in his Ford Bronco, a vehicle he had refinanced after the transmission went bad and had to be replaced.

Sacker and Toots, in their long-sleeve flannel shirts and overalls, took turns washing and then driving Mark's convertible into the village. Once, as a family, in Stanton, they bonded together in a lobster-eating contest. On a Sunday evening, when there was a mist but the moon was full, they drove the Bronco into the juniper flatlands back of home to where there was a strong smell of bog and rotting blueberries and the men attempted to call a moose. In response they heard only the howls of brush wolves. "A change in the weather can make all the difference," Toots said. (A month later Sacker would write off that vehicle when he ran over a moose on the highway. He had been on his way to Saint John to attend a George Jones concert.) They drank Scotch whisky and rum from paper bags, chewed tobacco and inhaled snuff, and smoked the roll-your-own cigarettes. With Mama-Jo they listened to *The Gospel Hour* on the plastic radio in the kitchen and then they played catch with a sad-eyed mongrel dog whose name was Comeback.

The next evening, wearing his old cowboy hat and boots, Toots taught Pam how to drive the pickup, standard shift, with a pencil sketch of the gears on the seat between them. And he showed her how to shoot Mark's Winchester rifle.

"Hold the butt-end tight to your shoulder," he said. "And don't jerk the trigger – squeeze. Have the shot surprise you."

He also told her that it was bad luck to walk under a loaded clothesline, and to tell your night dreams before breakfast. Later the family sat, long into the night, by a shore blaze where they drank Moosehead ale and sang campfire songs. The September night was cool, and Pam had to go to the house to find a windbreaker.

"It reminds me of an evening I spent with school mates in Grand Bend," she said.

Sacker, encouraged from the booze, played a few fiddle tunes he said that he had written himself, repeating and repeating his favourite phrases, many of which he would have heard on the radio, and which seemed to exhaust all of Mama-Jo's patience. She went into the house and the screen door slammed. As Sacker staggered to keep from falling into the flames, Toots ran through the guitar chords to the "St. Anne's Reel" and the "Fisher's Hornpipe," each with a twist and slightly off key, as he held the fiddle down on his elbow. And the fact that Sacker fancied himself as a showman was an embarrassment to Mark – that in his ears the homogeny of habit had long since reduced this music to silence, if not foolery. But he laughed and applauded in kindness.

For a moment he envisioned himself in his brother's shoes, drunk and yielding to the old need to display his talent. And suddenly he could see clearly why he went away. He thought, When we are insecure, we show off. We want to be seen, and try things we should not try and make fools of ourselves. The different periods in our lives resurface in our kin. But while he could see the simplicity in his earthy brother – the easy road he had chosen, or perhaps had fallen into – he knew he would always defend him.

After a drink and without music, Papa-Jo sang one of his old railroad songs, from the days when he travelled the boxcar circuit. Mark could remember him doing this in the fish camps after a drink of chokecherry wine.

Mark used to think he was misunderstood around home, because as he grew, he would not follow the local mindset, not be content to stay in the workday of farm and woods, the old bravado. Because he was small and with different goals, he had pleaded his indifference, partially to impress Mama-Jo, who had encouraged him to reach higher, because she felt that he had potential. He knew that she believed he was a different person than he really was, had encouraged not him but the son she felt he could be, to do great things if he applied himself. And so with great pain and lost love, he moved on from the family circle. Now, all these things came back to him in the tunes his brothers were playing, and which he had played on the fiddle as a boy. And like Jude Fawley's dream of getting to Christminster in Hardy's *Jude the Obscure*, suddenly Mark thought that maybe it would take more than one generation to swing it all around.

After a few more drinks, Sacker told Pam and Mark that he would be a professional musician and a comedian someday, become more famous than Jesus Christ.

And Papa-Jo said, "We all drink too much, but Sacker *really* drinks too much!"

"Papa-Jo says I don't make no sense. Well, I'll show him and Mickey too," Sacker said.

"Mickey has big dreams," Papa-Jo said. "But they are getable. He goes after things."

"I'm goin' after mine too, just watch me, Papa. I'll be rich and famous someday."

"When Sacker is drinking he believes his own bullshit," Toots said. And then as if to raise his own profile, added, "Properly speaking." And he laughed at his attempt to show some erudition. It was a harsh mocking laugh: "Ha ha, ha haaa." To keep it from spilling, he was cradling an opened bottle of rum between his legs.

Mark found that when Sacker was drinking – and most often he was, especially in the evenings – there was a feeling of unease that could spoil a party. To keep it smooth they asked him to play, because if neglected he would become angry and say, "Fuck you all! I guess I know what I'm talking about here." And this put an end to the merriment. Now he could feel some of this with Toots as well.

In the old days Mark took Sacker's declamations as a show of genius, or originality. And he encouraged him to work hard with his music. But later, he saw that his brother had not pursued a dream, and understood why. He was earthy and without direction, his virtue being his ability to follow, and to hold his drinks. Or perhaps Mark had himself grown. He never looked upon life as an entertainment, but as an opportunity to bring himself and the family to a higher standard. Why make a fool of yourself for a few laughs, why bring degradation to the family? He thought, We are seen as fools enough already.

Pam sat on the ground in the lotus position, swaying back and forth, dreamy-eyed, her hands clapping with the music. She appeared oblivious to everything outside the moment.

"This is the most fun I've had in my life. No wonder you want to move back home," she said.

"I told you so."

"They go out of their way to do fun things with us. Is it always like this?"

"Oh yes. I knew you would like it here. This is the real thing. There are no pretensions, no social climbing, not like in Niagara-on-the-Lake. Everyone keeps it simple, stays in the groove, helps one another to have a good time, that's what it's all about."

But for Mark, when he looked deep, it was a case of being back, listening to the same old crap, doing the things he struggled so hard to grow away from. In grade eight he had quit school to help his father in the woods, had grubbed potatoes from the mud, chopped stove wood, milked cows, and, yes, fiddled at house parties. And now, in the reliving of these experiences, came the old dogma of being looked down upon by the people from town whom he really wanted to be around.

For a moment he thought about heading back to Ontario, where no one would know if he made it or not, but from where he could claim bragging rights for having had the guts to move, and succeed in the eyes of the family and cousinhood by sending a little money home. They would never know the hardship he went through that first summer away. They would never know he had slept in a cousin's '59 Chevy, used the public washrooms at the Penn Centre Mall, bathed in a polluted Lake Ontario while he sandblasted the Queenston-Lewiston Bridge. They would never know he had worked the long day shovelling hot asphalt on a paving gang, or selling shoes in Grantham Plaza for room and board, before finally getting steady employment in the factory and a union membership. He had not mentioned these hardships in the letters he had written to Mama-Jo. And he knew, too, that if he moved back east, all those sacrifices would be in vain. He would have to start from scratch, possibly at the pulp mill in town.

To live here again I would have to be downriver, near Bradford, he thought. A poet is considered to be a thinker. That is the posterity I want. And if I write from the heart, my work won't be provincial. And then he contemplated, Or would I be like Sacker with his fiddle, showing off to get attention? He thought, I am drinking tonight; I'm drinking like I did in the last days before I went away. I have to keep my mouth shut, my plans hidden. He got up, staggered, and then sat down again. There it is, he thought. I'm back where I started!

Mark knew that to live back here and be different would take a lot of hard work, and that he would suffer putdowns from his people – except Mama-Jo, who always encouraged him to move on and be his true self – and he wondered if he had what it took to improve his station in life while living on the home river. If I make one mistake I will be labelled a fool, he thought. The local man is never given credit for anything, especially if he thinks differently. He is always an oddball, especially if he is writing poetry on his days off from work. An artist is never a success in his own time and country anyway. Mark had read that somewhere.

"They want us to move back. They want me to become one of them, you one of us," Mark told Pam. "No one likes a big shot, and they will work hard to keep this from happening to one of their own, even though they want to be seen travelling with me because I have been away and made some positive things happen. Mama-Jo pushed me harder than the others."

Pam said, "They don't want to see you become prominent, even as they hang onto your coattails for prominence."

"To be one of them is to be content with the life and not reach higher."

"That might not be so bad. The stakes would be low, less pressure on you."

It was easy for Mark to persuade Pam to persuade him to move back, so easy it frightened him. It was like crawling back into a comfortable old bed with a squeaky groove. And he felt a touch of guilt for letting it happen, because on the surface it would be her idea. And it would also be her fault if things did not work out. But being from away, she would not be to blame, not like he would if the decision was his, as he knew the old routine. So he told people, "I made it good in Ontario, but I guess Pam wants me to move here to live. What can I do?"

Pam does not realize that despite first impressions, a place, once lived in is no longer the same country, Mark thought. But I know this land and its shortfalls. And by Christ, I can show this river what I can do if I put my mind to it. It won't be easy, but I'll do it for Mama-Jo. And then he thought, That sounded a bit like one of Sacker's declarations. But the difference is, I will work hard to make it happen. Just you watch me!

It would take a few years before Mark realized that to be a success, he did not have to show the community anything. This is about digging down deep inside myself, he thought, to find the real *me* and achieving the goals that please me. Only then can I truly live up to that potential Mama-Jo, in her loving heart, always encouraged.

WILD BLUEBERRIES

THE STUBBORN BLUEBERRY BUSH THRIVED IN CLEARINGS, or where there had been a grass or forest fire. (In that regard they reminded me of my mother's will to endure, even succeed in the outlands that was our farm.) The berry leaves were a stiff, waxen brown, their tangled stems like kinked wire – apple trees for elves, or perches for a butterfly. At first there had been clusters of little purple buds, and then the bag-like white bells, each with a per-fumed clapper of rose-like delicacy – male and female – their petals having survived the last frosts of spring. The blossoms, which bees impregnated by the millions, were followed in June by the prayer-bead-size green berries, in hard clumps of three or four, that when tasted were so tangy they made my jaws ache and brought tears to my eyes. But I ate them, leaves and all, like I did with the red tea berries and the white moss berries that tasted like mint. These were a kind of farm boy's candy, a secret not to be shared with town kids, symbols of the new season. To me, a wild blueberry, long before it ripened, tasted better than the mature ber-ry did in a pie or a jar, even when sugar was added – especially when sugar was added. I had a sour tooth.

(How often I have said that an acquired taste has to do with childhood, and our becoming independent in the tanginess we choose to like, even if it is bitter. We stand up for it. So that when we grow old, we long for that childish flavour that is so filled with the desires and ambitions of our youth. I suppose the same can be said of music, even bad melodies, in that they move us internally, because of the youthful feeling and dreams therein.)

As a young lad on my way to and from school, I looked for green blueberries by the roadside and along the railway tracks where there had been a lot of sleeper fires. In places, the bushes grew up into the page-wire gates and pushed toward the white gravel rail bed. As summer advanced, the berries changed from green to purple, and then to blue/black, with a covering of gray powdery railroad dust, their thin ebony skin a pearl-colour inside. Some of them grew as big as marbles, each with a little gaping eye – with open lashes – on the blossom end and on the stem end, a navel. When a sparrow flew out of the bracken, I looked for its nest and found the tiny blue eggs that were also full of life. Motherhood was everywhere.

As well, blueberries grew in the schoolyard, the cow pasture, and the big woods where the bushes were taller and the berries, though fewer, were as big as a winter crab apple, all free for the picking. For a time in high summer, they were a source of income for me. I gathered and sold them – in bootleg fashion for twenty-five cents a bucket – to my great-uncle at his store in the village, who in turn, when we went there to shop, gave them to my mother for making preserves. For me, it was money to buy candy, a soda, an ice cream cone, or later on, a cigarette. My friend Carroll, who lived in the village, always picked enough berries to pay her way into the carnival that came in August to the Catholic Fairgrounds.

I can remember being in the fields on July evenings, swatting insects at their lively tunes amid the shrilling of grasshoppers while sitting among the clusters of shrub, separating the blueberries from the greens, while filling a bucket to the brim and beyond. I can also recall going there, barefoot, on bright summer mornings after a shower – when the scent of the woods, the hazel bush, and thyme were strongest – and sitting among the little nettles that were clinging with silver raindrops, while filling my tin dipper. The berries became glued together from the moisture. They stained my hands a deep purple – the way that berries bleed, like froth overflowing from a stew pot – before I carefully made my way back to the house, in wet trousers, brushing my dirty feet on the rush doormat, to give my yield directly to mother, who was making muffins.

And during those long summer rains before the hay was cut, when the fog obscured the view of our distant barn that was hunched down in the long grass, in the outside kitchen of our tree-shaded farmhouse, my mother and I huddled around the wood stove, absorbing the blueberry aromas, while looking out the window for an evening pink sky as we waited and prayed for a sunny day to follow. I carried wood from the yard, digging down into the pile for dry maple sticks that were the right size for Mum to feed into the firebox and bring the oven to the temperature she need-ed for the baking. On the oven door she tested the piecrust's inner texture with a straw from the broom.

But we had gone to the railway first, my mother and I, to get enough berries to make a pie. (It had been a clear day and the whole countryside was filled with promise, a church bell ringing in that faraway village.) I remember Mum, in a low-cut sundress, under a big straw hat, kneeling among the shrubs, as we filled a small bucket. She praised me for being such a fast picker and for the cleanness of the berries I gathered. In the simplicity of child-hood, this approval inspired me to work harder, to become known in the household as a go-getter, but more, I think, to please her, as she was sensitive to my unspoken thoughts, which of course were always favourable to her wishes – wanting to see me succeed at whatever I did. Though not a teacher by trade, she had a way of encouraging me with compliments. She once told me that sen-sitivity and talent were the most important virtues anyone could have, that learning and genius were two different things, and that intellect could be gotten from books. "Imagination is more impor-tant than knowledge," she said. "Be true to yourself, follow your heart." Having been self-taught – though a good reader – she had a certain disdain for academia and associated it with snobbery. She had a pedigree that could not be captured on paper, or worn on a sleeve.

As a widowed farm woman, she walked barefoot in the river meadows, drank brook water, while scenting the blueberry bush in bloom, as she looked under the big low-branched trees for the cows that she milked daily. I remember seeing her, a dairy maid in a white linen apron. In a yoke, she carried the heavy buckets from the pasture to our milk house, which was built over the spring and where the cream separator stood. Later, as she pumped the churn's dasher in our lamp-lit kitchen, she sang "One Morning in May," an English folk balled I had often heard my great-uncle play on his homemade flute.

Mother's shrill colour tones, shaped by her beautiful soul, her moments of melancholy that were so full of tenderness, were meant for her ears only, yet her voice reached outside the house where I listened with glee. She would never know that this small display of intimacy brought us so close together – as did the colours in my father's paintings, long after he went to France to fight in World War II. Daddy was killed there in 1944 and is buried in Flanders with a little white cross marking his grave. Because I was only three when he went overseas, I can remember my father more from photographs than the man himself: the wedding picture that hung on our living room wall and, above it, the one of him in uniform he sent home: Private Daniel Watson, of the Royal New Brunswick Regiment, North Shore.

And in the future, which is the true measure of art, the way that little moments stand up in country life, I can still see Mother's black hair falling over her eyes, as she made butter, then went back to the barn where, on a threshing floor, she flailed the bean pods, before going to where there was a wind to winnow them, the chaff scattering over the stubble land. (It had been all in a day's work.) Beyond the gate, where the tree branches and hay ricks turned to gold in the sunset, sunflowers stood with bowed heads, their long open lashes weeping, as if out of shame for my mother's plight. But she was happy in her world, and while being attractive in youth – she had a radiant smile – in old age she claimed dignity and grace.

Now as the morning went on, Mother became quiet, as if she were lost in thought, or had been set free to be with nature, unbound from the routine of farm chores – she could justify her berry-gatherings as work – for this outing. And sensing her melancholy – for I could read *her* thoughts too – I kept silent. There among the wild blueberry bushes, along that railway line, with its old-world charm, the hobo smells of sun-heated gravel, rusted steel, and weathered telegraph poles, the only sounds were that far-off church bell, the chirp of a sparrow, or perhaps the snap and crack of steel, a train approaching. I put a penny on a rail and watched as it was flattened by the big iron wheels, the train whistle echoing through those berried hills. And for a moment, I wanted to become, not a gatherer, not a botanist, but a railwayman – those electrifying, short-lived dreams of youth that would never see fruition.

In her spare time, my mother sometimes sketched, without pretentions, the little farm scenes with which she was so familiar: the old apple tree in blossom, the farm wagon at harvest, a clothes-line laden with red stockings, or a patch quilt of many colours. Sometimes she pencilled her own portrait in reflection from a bedroom mirror. (I still have one of these.) And she always emphasized the importance of imagination and solitude if we were to be good artists, saying that every painter is, while she is painting, a painter of her own self, and that her work is merely an instrument that she presents to the viewer to help him or her see a part of themselves they would otherwise be indifferent to. Like a composer of classical music takes us on a journey inside ourselves.

I now wish that an artist could have been with us to capture the scene that I carry inside me: mother and child gathering berries along the railroad. Because there was something captivating about the moment which had a spirit of its own – the sun shining down on my mother's flowered dress and straw hat, beneath which her hair was in a single plait, her arms sunburned, the parallel rails that extended beyond view, to bigger and more exciting places. And there was the purple shade of the trees beyond the fence, the cattle bars we had crawled under, the drifting white clouds as fluffy as down in the unfathomable blue sky. Because these things could not be recaptured later on, save for a brief glimpse in my nostalgic mind, when the inspiration was triggered by the smell of woodsmoke, the taste of a blueberry, or the melody of that little folk song my mother sang when she worked the churn. Back then, like the railway, my life's imaginings stretched so far into the future I could see no end to them. It is thus today in looking back, in that nostalgia enhances the illusions of juvenile dreams.

For me, from that time on, the image of Mother, on her knees, meditating, while unconsciously putting blueberries into her overflowing tin, became frozen in time, like the figures we see in school books, old curios in a cabinet, symbols on an urn, or the plaster of Paris angels we made in vocational Sunday school. Real or imagined, they stayed with me through life.

Folks said that, in the autumn of her years, my mother looked like Queen Elizabeth II: hunch-shouldered in a royal blue dress, imitation pearl beads, and with a wide-brimmed hat over her steel-gray hair. And to me, she was just as dignified. Though poor monetarily, and having never known the fulfilment of a school graduation or an award citation, she always showed signs of grandeur; she was my queen and teacher in that she made things happen. While I knew her as majestic – like country music is invisible to city folk – the rest of the community, the village, knew her as a no-nonsense figure who was a deep thinker and full of emotion. With her delicate features and sensitive qualities, it was like she was better suited to a more cultivated environment, perhaps as a violinist or pianist. Having been a chambermaid in her youth, she had a taste for the finer city things of life. But of course she would never leave the farm. On Sundays after church, on our oilcloth-covered dining room table, she set a glass pitcher of homemade lemonade, around which stood a circle of crystal drinking glasses, a custom she had picked up in town.

At that summertime of year, our old country home – my mother's castle – was serene, the curtains having been drawn, awnings cranked down, and with the cooking fires being in the adjacent, shed-like summer kitchen. The place was also kept cool by the big river elms. And I can remember feeling the cold linoleum floors under my bare feet as I dressed, went down the stairs, and out through a breezeway to have breakfast. There was tea brewing, the scent of bread baking in the oven of the wood range – smells that mixed with the radio's country songs, while I ate my sugarless porridge. And later, no matter where I travelled, or the places I owned, I could never find that same atmosphere, or the grandeur and respect that my mother demanded in that old gray-shingled farmhouse with busied wall sketches, plank kitchen table, and the hand-hewn whitewashed beams. It was like the first reaction I got as a child from a fairy tale or a nursery rhyme, in that along the way, it could never be recaptured with the same nuance and passion as of old.

These childhood metaphors still take me back to those summer mornings that were all too short-lived. By the railway line, filling a tin dipper with blueberries, one by one, seemed like a lifetime of minor events, a sequence of moments that would eventually lead to a whole: the illusion of what life could be if I listened to my mother, kept focused, worked hard to fulfil my youthful dreams. Or later in the purchase of something with the money earned – which was always less gratifying than the dream had been, the togetherness we shared in making it happen – so that the memories of the outings, be they weeks apart, jelled into one major symbol that was unconsciously set down for posterity. I can still see and feel it from both sides: the image of Mother on her knees in the fields, with one hand on top of her hat to keep the breeze from blowing it away, when she looked like a peasant woman we might see in a classical painting; or in our winter kitchen, with the overlighted birthday cake she decorated for me when I turned eighteen, and her tears, and the sentimental goodbye that followed.

By that time, the idea of spending a summer morning picking blueberries had become a boring and ingeniously time-wasting occupation, an out-of-date custom. For once you outgrow a thing, you can never go back to it literally and expect the same emotions to be waiting there; indeed when a person has reached adolescence and beyond, he will seldom remain a hostage to his boyhood – or his mother. He wants to be in the city where less tedious, more exciting things are happening, and in bigger measure. By this time, too, my taste in things, and indeed my dreams as well, had changed to something more sophisticated. (And I often wondered as to what depth my mother's early longings – the perceived extension of her future – had been fulfilled or if she had ever outgrown them as she appeared so happy on the farm.) And the blueberry fields, the fulfilment of the great harvest, the little berried steps toward maturity, plus the excitement I had imagined to be on the far end of that lonesome railway line (also a great disappointment later on) became something I could never go back to, not with the same gradation as of old.

And how, at times, I longed for that kind of stamina, that kind of eagerness, that kind of contentment to return, if only in some small measure.

Until one day (January 14, 2001) when the winter rains were coming down and there was a threat of snow in the wind. Getting word that my mother was terminally ill, I left Sherbrook on an eastbound train, observing the woodlands along the berried tracks – she was still pictured there – arriving home well after midnight, to be with her at the time of her death. After being away, this time for just six months, I went to her bedside in what had, through the years, become a dispirited and dilapidated farmhouse – my old home and her castle. In her overdecorated and medicine-smelling bedroom, I held her frail hands, spoke to her in the old home jargon. But she was not responding to my words. Instead she was pinching me with a bone-crushing grip, and whispering, "Oh, Dan, you have come home at last to be with me as you promised so long ago! Oh, Dan, I always knew you were alive and that you would come home someday. Dan, please help me get through this awful pain!"

It was as if she were still a young woman and I (Dan) had a remedy for her suffering. And shortly the nurse arrived and gave her a needle filled with morphine. In her state of delirium, she had taken me for my father. And I grieved to think that she did not remember me, her own son, rather Daddy, who had left so long before I did, and that his leaving had impacted her so much more. As I said, the most important things in life stand up the longest. But the pain in her eyes made me realize that her indifference toward me was not personal, but the result of a much greater sorrow in earlier times. She had never been one to go to the Cenotaph and cry on Remembrance Day, and was bashful when she had to sit in a front pew of the church. She had kept it all hidden, as country women will. I did not attempt to tell her I was Jim, thinking it was more important for her to be with her true love just now, a man whose brown eyes I had inherited. But our hands were locked in a firm grip and she was staring into my eyes, with those clear blue eyes of hers that were now glassed over from the pain and medication, until her breathing changed, and there was a great rattle in her chest. Her grip strengthened and then relaxed and I could feel the spirit and the great soul leave her broken and demented body. And she was gone physically from this world.

Not until I reached the frailty of old age – once a man, twice a boy – after the railroad bed had been turned into a bicycle trail, life was gone from those fields that would never be planted again, and the farmhouse had been devoured by the prospects of industrialization, could I see it clearly. As Anton Chekhov wrote, "Every idea materializes gradually in its own time." In life as in art, distance is the true qualifier.

Now in my longings to get back to the old home place, if only metaphorically, I try to relate a hot summer morning, the taste of a wild blueberry, or the lyrics of an old country song to my youth. But I find that in going over those fallow lands with a fine-tooth comb, the strongest images are of Mother, not from her deathbed exactly, not from an old wedding photograph, but from the blueberry fields – a living monument on her knees, dressed the way she was in the straw hat and sundress, the smiling blueberry-coloured eyes, the sun beaming down on her as if from heaven.

AT OAK POINT

IN LATE AUGUST JOHNNY INVITED ME TO ONE OF HIS staff parties. At first I was reluctant to go, but decided I would be a sport, go along, shake a few hands, and help nourish his banking career. Besides, I wanted to see what was going on at those frequent – after work – gatherings, if possible, without revealing my inner sufferings in the process. He had been making me feel old-fashioned and somewhat of an introvert. I wondered what the office staff knew as to his shenanigans and how they would treat me. Would it be with disdain or would they be patronizing? Certainly it would be a way to read what he had been saying about me at the bank. And I wondered too if there was any gossip circulating among his group as to a bathtub incident that he was rumoured to have had with a female employee.

The party would be held at the bank manager's cottage on the coast. Johnny said, "Everyone has to take a bottle of booze and something to eat. And I'm warning you that you might not like this kind of a get-together."

"Sounds like whoever is having the event wants everyone else to pay for it. When I have a party, I tell people to not bring anything, that I'll supply the food and drinks."

"Look, if you want to pass up the invitation, I'll understand."

"No, no I'd like to go! I've been here alone, doing housework and gardening all summer. It's time I got out of the house. Plus I'd like to meet your friends."

After showering, I put on one of Johnny's long denim shirts

and was brushing my hair at the kitchen mirror. "I wonder if the night will be too cold to wear shorts."

"Yes, it's too cold for shorts. There will be a heavy frost by morning."

Later, as Johnny drove the River Road with the top down, I sat with my window cranked up and a sweater thrown over my shoulders. There was no conversation. He played the k.d. lang CD *I'm Crying Over You* too loud, like you hear in parades and which I found embarrassing when we drove past the houses of acquaintances.

Along that road that followed the edge of the bay, I observed the scenery: the weed-fringed pavement, with its yellow markings, the slanting shadows of the elm trees. Oak Point was where I had spent the night with David so long ago. He flashed in my mind and then was gone, back to Kingston's Military Academy. There was no room for him in my feelings just now. But I thought, What a quaint old countryside this is, with the noble elms and the little white houses that stand on cliffs so close to the water. It is very much the Maritime landscape that Longfellow wrote about. Then I thought, The Maritimes are such a wonderful place to live, the air is always so fresh here. I don't think I could live in Ontario, at least not the busy southern parts around Toronto. My neighbour Mrs. Hennessy's affection for that part of the country must be nostalgic, an illusion from her schooldays. I have the same protectiveness for the farm life upriver. But we must be careful with nostalgia. Like Wordsworth's pen, it paints a beautiful picture.

On the coast proper, Johnny pulled into a yard where a dozen cars were parked beside a weathered cottage. Cases of beer and food sat on picnic tables, and nearby there was a red, double-cab pickup truck with the driver's door open, its radio playing the song "Don't Worry, Be Happy." Across a small field out on the beach, against a backdrop of the sea, with its narrow band of pink sky on the horizon – which to me looked like the matting on a canvas seascape – a fire burned in a pit around which some people sat on nylon chairs and held branches supporting marshmallows into the blaze. At first glance this reminded me of a photo of a whaler's campfire I had seen in *National Geographic*.

For an instant the smell of the fire, the snap and crack of burning pitch in the white spruce logs took me back to when I had quit school and lunched in the woods with Daddy. Together, at the boiling hole as we had lunch, we listened to the melancholy cries of the moose-bird, a spirit of the old woodsmen that came to eat out of our hands, the same notes repeating themselves and repeating themselves – musicians who had no hopes of reaching higher on the scales and thus rendered their redundant little tune through life. They were like us, the simple music, the lifeless Saturday nights on the farm. I wondered if they would still be in that place, but guessed they would, if climate change had not killed them.

I thought of how my father could tell the weather by the crackle and snap of a campfire, the colour of the flame, the echoes the trees made, and the voices of birds. In spite of his ruggedness and lack of a book education, Daddy had many natural inclinations. He was closer to the land than anyone I knew and could spot a phony a mile away.

"Always be yourself; follow your own internal instincts in love or otherwise," he told me. "The hell with how it looks to others."

There was always a comforting ghost in the fragrance of the burning wood. There was also a soothing in the murmur of waves that lapped upon the sand, the restless evening breeze making the water gasp and ebb, although these sounds and the scent of decayed seaweed carried no messages, as I had grown up inland and had no memory of them, except on that one night with David. And I refused to let my mind go there, because I did not want to distort that teen image with this tormented return. I would force myself to stay in the here and now.

Johnny introduced me around and, as suspected, I was accepted into the group with a detectable indifference. As his friends tried to accommodate me, or pretended to, I glimpsed his new lover's flashing eyes, which were the colour of the sea, recognized her smoker's raspy voice from phone calls to the house. (It had to be her because she had an apartment on Jane Street, which was near enough to the bank for lunch meetings. I had heard rumours of them being in a bathtub together and, seeing the chemistry between them, I could see this happening.) And I was saddened by the fact that I was no longer a true part of Johnny's circle. His boss, Gil, who was over-friendly, greeted me with artificial warmth while giving me a full glass of cheap Scotch whisky which appeared to be straight from the bottle. This man I recognized by sight, having seen him about town, and knew him to be an arrogant son of a bitch. There will be no sense of truth in this group, I thought. No in-depth conversation here tonight.

"So how are things going out at the old farmhouse?" Gil asked without looking at me.

"The farmhouse?"

"Yeah, that big old place you got out there in the boondoggles."

"My home in Howard! It's still mostly in the planning stages, I'm afraid."

"Hitting the books, writing some poetry, gardening, I hear?"

"A bit, yes a bit."

"Having dropped out of high school, it must be embarrassing to sit in a classroom with a dozen women looking to upgrade their teacher's certificates . . . I mean, it takes courage to go into a place like that. I got to hand it to you, Sally. I'd be afraid of looking like a total fool, myself. Plus there is no money in it, not for someone interested in gardening and the arts."

"It's not about money. I like to learn new things. And I can hold my own among them."

"We have to follow our life's dreams, I guess."

"That's how I see it."

"And some professor from Ontario liked your poems, I hear?"

"That's what he said in a letter."

"It's always good to have a friend in the business."

"Yes, I need that, I guess."

A short man in a t-shirt, and with hairy arms, approached me. I had not seen him before. "So how's all that stuff going out on the farm with the big garden and all the reading?"

"Ahh, everything's going fine, thanks." I moved toward the fire where I sat warming my hands. I felt that these people were all too interested in my career for bank workers who probably couldn't tell me who wrote *War and Peace*. So I kept my answers short, smiled, and sipped my drink while trying to keep from falling off a chair that had one bad leg. As the chair buckled and sagged on one side, the pink-stripped horizon shifted and I was looking at it from a slant so that it resembled a framing on the wall that needed to be straightened upright. It was obvious they were trying to get me drunk, having me sprawling on the grass under a faulty chair. And I wondered what kind of an oddball Johnny had described me as.

For a brief moment I felt naive and defenceless. I wondered if they would try to assassinate me spiritually, think they could knock that eager-to-learn spirit out of me. For them, because I'd had a strong drink and because I had never worked in town, they would see me as easy pickings. They would be reaching for the top of a cherry tree growing in a hollow, trying to sample the best of-ferings, otherwise beyond reach. I had had my occasional shot of single malt at home, at bedtime, but felt my little Saturday night ritual was kept in the family's confidence. Now, I wondered if this was the case. Why did this man give me whisky without ask-ing what I liked to drink, and in such an overfilled tumbler? Why had he set me on a bad chair? It was to be analyzed. In fact, every-thing that had been said so far was to be examined in some way or another. This I would do tomorrow while working in the garden. But for now I had to try hard to be a good sport, not show even a slight hint of jealousy toward the woman I suspected of sleeping with my husband.

Some cormorants flew in a long wavering string, yellow at first and then black as they dropped against the low sky, to circle and light on the water and form another canvas.

"It must be hard for a woman to look after a big garden all day, and spend her evenings with her head in a book," a young man remarked.

"Yes, I suppose it would be," I said.

"What are you studying right now?"

"Who, me? Nothing at the moment, I'm at a party," I said and laughed. I felt like saying, I'm studying a fool, but thought better of it. While I had been told that I had a child's sensitiveness, I had learned years before how to take a few shots and keep smiling. But I thought, What do you suppose Johnny has been saying about me to these people? Has he been making me appear as a relic so that when he does walk out, he will have had a good excuse? I looked around and felt like I was outclassed, outnumbered, and sitting in a pit of snakes. And I wondered why Johnny had brought me. Did he do it to show his fellow bank workers what an eccentric he had married? Or was it to show *her* the contrast between his world and mine?

As we sat around the fire and the conversation went from mortgage rates, to property taxes, to mutual funds, to baseball, and back to mortgage rates, Gil came with the bottle and splashed more six-year-old Scotch into my glass. I took a sip, to prove that I was not a square and could party with them. The pink matting on the horizon tilted again and I had to struggle not to fall off the sagging chair. I steadied the drink. The moods of the sky and sea were changing now – fleeting and contradictory – as was the instability of the setting, the uncertainty of its outcome. A person would have to be really drunk to stay here for very long, listen to the bullshit, I thought. I'd like to hit that big cocksucker Gil with a backhand slap, watch him go down on his arse in the water. "Yes, in the water," I said out loud and laughed to myself at the thought. It was then my chair buckled completely and I was sprawling on my knees, spilling the drink on my blouse. For a moment the tilted sea (an inky blue with its pink matting) was above me, the tall blades of grass pointing downward in reflection, and now with the taste of sea sand in my teeth. My first thought was, I'm so glad I did not wear shorts.

But my mind and body had already switched to automatic. "Jesus! Who pushed me?"

I got up swinging, and seeing that no one was near, kicked the aluminium chair into a cluster of shrubs. I picked it up and beat it against a rock until it was a crumple of tin pipes and nylon threads. "That chair's a fucking death trap," I puffed.

It was a scene that made everyone laugh.

"Kick the son of a whore again," someone shouted. "He's getting up!"

"That's how we get rid of our old lawn furniture up on the farm," Johnny said with a giggle and a smirk.

"That's how you fight at the dances too," another chided.

And I thought, There goes the beautiful image I had of Oak Point.

Johnny came over and brushed the sand from my blouse. "No one pushed you," he whispered. "And no one forced you to drink like that either."

Johnny is right, I thought. I'm getting drunk, acting the fool like I used to do in Glenn Falls, away back before I ever met him. For a moment I felt sorry for Johnny, that he had made a mistake and the fact that he now had to go to these extremes to find happiness, and among such outlandish and loathsome people. I asked myself, had I driven him to it, while shielding myself, through my art, from the loneliness of real country life, so he had turned to the town circle for compassion?

"Oh God, I am such a criminal," I said to myself. "What have I done to poor Johnny?" What have I done to me, again? These are not real people. And that is why he is no longer real, not in any way the man I married. I was feeling lower than I could ever remember, even in the old days on the farm when there was absolutely nothing to do on Saturday nights, a despair that had me considering suicide. Now, I have killed the once beautiful spirit of Johnny Morgan, all because of my own selfishness.

But Daddy said I had to be myself, do my own thing, no matter how it looks to others. Then I thought, Who was Daddy but a farmer/woodsman? How would he act among such people? They would cut him up.

I must not go back there, I thought. I must keep that old day locked away in a secure package and not open it again. It grieves me to think that from this point on, the memories of the coast will be of this night and not the former. What I felt with my first love had been heartache, yes, even when we were together, so in love with him was I, so unsure was I of myself.

I tried to imagine the Johnny Morgan I married being a friend to these people as they sat by the fire with their eyes trained on me in a down-home kind of interrogation, as I had done before I met David and whose short-lived acceptance had driven me away from that circle, away from the upriver clan. For a brief moment I understood these people and was on their side, having fun with a newcomer, who did not know the local way of thinking, the pulse of town life. And I wondered if my indifference to that circumstance was the reason why Johnny – now one of them, or pretending to be, to keep his job – was pursuing a new woman. It was obvious he wanted out of our marriage and was no longer in my corner. He had never liked the farm, the big old house – he wanted a brick bungalow in town. Sure, why wouldn't he?

"Her taste seems older than she really is," I overheard a man say. "It's not like she's some big shot from away."

"It's called maturity," another mumbled.

"She's just a hillbilly from up Glenn Falls way, that's all she is."

"Originally, yes."

"Then how did she get so goddamned yuppie . . ."

"Books."

I looked at the circle of faces, reflecting orange from the burning softwood, and Johnny was not in the group. I pretended not to notice, but visions of a Saturday night in Glenn Falls a hundred years ago flashed before me and my face caught on fire.

I thought, Now what do you suppose is going on here? I stood nursing my empty glass and my heart ached. Oh God, why did I come? Why did I let Johnny put me through this?

I staggered toward the house where I knew there were bottles of water on a picnic table. And the field tilted under my feet so at times I had to reach for the grass and hold on.

"Sally, where ya goin'?" Gil hollered.

"I'm talking to a fool right now!" I muttered.

"Whaaattt?"

"What did you ask me?"

"I asked where you're going."

"I'm getting a drink of water."

My head was spinning, like having overslept, I had awakened, still dreaming. Near the house, Johnny was talking to the blue-eyed woman I had been introduced to as Judy Craig. They were not touching, but sitting close on a bench.

"Look! It's Sally!" Judy said in a too-loud voice. And then, "Whatta ya lookin' for, Sally?"

Judy had not brought her husband to the party.

"I'm getting a drink of water," I said. I was thinking, What a desperate feeling it is to be depending on the other woman, a total stranger, to leave you with a shred of dignity.

Johnny said, "Wait, I'll get you a drink."

"No, no. I can get myself a drink."

He came to the table, found a bottle of water, unscrewed the top, and passed it to me.

"Look. I think I'd like to go home now," I said.

"What? Go home? But it's only . . ."

"I know, but I'd like to go home now if you don't mind."

"I guess we're going home," Johnny said to Judy. "I knew I shouldn't have brought this lady. She goes to bed with the birds."

I went to sit in Johnny's car. I sat alone for a long time, my inner life broken. I could hear the laughter from the fireside. These are good people, I thought. These poor souls would not know any better. They wouldn't know how to be nice, or who to be nice to, so I must forgive them. But it is sad when a gathering like this and with this agenda is someone's idea of a party.

Finally, Johnny came, got into the car, and slammed the door. He had an opened beer bottle standing between his legs. And his chomping cigar switched from side to side, then stopped in the centre of his face. Without speaking he started the engine. Spinning the tires, he backed out the driveway and drove silently toward home, the night breeze blowing my hair about, the same loud k.d. lang music playing. He kept glancing in the rear-view mirror at lights that followed.

I turned to see Judy in her red double-cab pickup, following close. There's something spooky about this, I thought. Something is rotting in the state of Denmark.

When we were almost home, Johnny pulled over and stopped the car.

Judy drove up behind us with the high beams projecting on me and Johnny. Leaving the engine running, the music playing, Johnny got out and went back to lean on the driver's door where he talked to her for what seemed like an hour. I was cold and wished I had brought a heavy coat. I kicked the CD player and the music stopped. I thought of getting behind the wheel, driving on home without him. But thought better of it, because I felt that was what he wanted me to do. Then I would be to blame for driving away and leaving him on the side of the highway. As cars went past and folks I knew honked and waved, I thought, How must this look to the people of my community?

I tooted the horn. After some time, I honked again. I opened my door as if to go back, confront them. I would grab the wheel wrench from the trunk. Take the windshield out of that truck. But then I thought, Drunk as I am, if Judy so desired, she could strike me dead. And I would be the criminal who attacked her with a deadly weapon.

Finally, Johnny came back, got into the car, and we drove into Howard. For a moment I breathed easier, but I could feel the lights that followed, like a hot breath against the back of my neck.

When we pulled into our driveway, I had to concentrate, slow down my breathing. And there was the threat of a migraine. I looked into Johnny's shiftless eyes and spoke slowly and deliberately, coughing to find my own solid pitch. "Thank you for a wonderful night. I will never go anywhere with you again as long as I live!"

He gave me a grin, and from this, I realized these were the words he had been pushing me to say. It would be me who started the slide, not him. Just as it had been me who wanted to get out of the farmhouse, go to a beach party, have some fun, because it was an August Saturday night.

THE STALK BURN

WE PUT OUR POTATO SEED IN THE GROUND ON THE twenty-fourth of May. They are soggy and freshly cut, each with at least one good eye. We carry them from the woodshed's open door where my grandfather sits on the long-shafted wheelbarrow with a galvanized pail between his knees, sizing up each potato and carving them into halves and quarters. This seed – after a hundred years in the family – our own special variety, is to be dropped, eyes up, one sandal track apart, in the newly turned furrows. As Father and I make the drills with the horse and cultivator, the boys and girls, having gotten a day from school to help with the planting, scatter the gritty fertilizer that sticks beneath their nails. At length, the whole concern is covered by the changing-coloured, new-turned soil, banked by the rusty mould boards. The children want to complete the task by early evening, so they can go fishing for trout in the eddy, which at this time of year we can smell from the potato lands. It is stronger than that of the horse and the loam. Beyond the tree-lined riverbank there is a combination of fragrances: water, a sprinkling of maple and cherry blossom, and fish. "Anyone can be a good fisher in May," Father says.

When we have finished planting in the early evening and the children gather worms and head to the shore, I borrow Father's car and go to the village to see my friend Catherine. She is new and quite unknown to me, and our possibilities together are larger than life. And I hope the relationship will grow accordingly. (Although she has warned me against getting too serious too soon, I have images of us walking down Main Street, with her in a white sundress, sandals, and a large straw hat, like the one that Natalie Wood wore in the movie *Splendor in the Grass*.)

The June rains come, for weeks on end, and the seed's progeny emerges – among scattered switch grasses and pigweed – first with a crack and then with a bulge, breaking through the rain-dimpled drills, with a knuckle and then a squirrel's ear of new leaf. This leads to the tiresome hours of helping Father cultivate the plants, turning old earth into new, walnut into mahogany. The mould boards bank, even cover, the plants, as the harness and the shafts of the horse-hoe squeak in the dust and flies. This is always done in the evening hours when the leaves press upward to catch the due. Afterwards, there is a quick shower – or a swim in the river – and a drive into the village as Catherine and I get to know one another. We go to the picture shows, eat at the diners. In the little time that it takes for the young, for me it is already true love.

At blossom time, the potato field became a giant flower garden, the abode of a million bees and other insects. The drills cover, as the plants reach across to embrace one another's limbs, as if for support. Eventually the field resembles a corrugated jungle, with its many inhabitants that dart among branches stretched in tangles across the other's dulse-like leaves. The leaves wither upon their greasy limbs, which hold the unearthed snarl of black twine that clings to the thin-skinned, egg-size potatoes if they have been pulled before their growth has ended. Until the movie house and the diner have shut down for the school season, and morning frost has turned the leaves to rust, and the stalks have collapsed into rows of brown spiders, made brittle by the wind and sun.

Digging time brings first the stalk-pulling and the carrying to drill side, the thyme-scented straw, and the hacking out of limbless little men, the brand of which, after so many generations, we know not well ourselves.

After we have hacked them from their bulging drills to the ring of iron diggers, clanging among the rocks, and the rakes are used standing to rest our backs upon with folded arms, the potatoes lay crowded in broad rows, exposed and naked to dry in the October sun. Again the children have stayed home from school to help, and they half-drag, half-swing the tiresome heavy buckets that overflow from having been dealt too few sacks to accommodate a drill's expected turnout, especially in the rich bottom lands. And the breeze is cool when we take off our sweaty fall jumpers.

After the burlap sacks are filled and tied with twine, like so many bulging duffle bags, they are piled upon the wooden drag-sled, until it creaks with strain, as the horse nods with digging hooves the heaps of lumpy produce to the farmhouse. The children scramble for seats on the load but tumble off with each nudge forward.

"Save a bag for Aunt Edith," Mother shouts as we empty the sacks with a rumble into a chute that hangs from a cellar window. "And one for the church supper," Father says, placing two sacks on the ground. At the supper last fall, a man from the church committee praised Father's potatoes. "They are nice and dry this year, Will," he shouted across the hall. How embarrassed we were when everyone suddenly looked at our table. But Father was proud, seeing his contribution, the labour of his many hours afield, being enjoyed by the town's folk.

Now, with the potatoes having been taken from the ground, the earth appears dry and warm with small granite rocks, and a few scarred or too-small potatoes, which the cows and the crows feast upon, dappling the levelled drills. Runner tracks loop among the many bunches of snapping dry potato stalks that stand in the field like so many cocks of rotting hay. "Why don't we burn the potato stalks tonight?" I ask.

"Yes," Father says. "They are dry enough and it could rain tomorrow. I heard a blue jay."

"And a spark flew out of the kitchen stove," Mother adds.

"And the river, we can smell it from the house!"

"Yes, yes! Let's burn tonight." The children emerge from their homework. "Why do we always have to wait for Halloween?"

As dusk approaches, we put on our coats and cotton gloves and after getting a two-pronged pitchfork from the barn, we set out across the darksome fields in advance of Father, who is hustling about the kitchen in search of matches. The thought of building a fire has the children high-stepping in eagerness. I can remember the feeling, the simplicity of childhood. And I envy them. It is the excitement that comes with going to do a thing, more than the experience itself. (Like every encounter imagined is better before it happens.) Now, I can only find that kind of elevation when I am on the road to the village; going to see Catherine; thinking of her, then sitting with her – hand in hand – kissing her lips and both eyes, on her dad's front veranda. In my case it has all been as good, even better, than the aforementioned illusions.

And then, on an evening in autumn, when the leaves had dropped from the trees and there was a threat of snow in the river wind, she held my hand, cried, and told me that she was moving on to a bigger community, bigger things, and I most likely would never see her again. And for a while I wondered, How do you learn to not trust someone you love? It is when they tell you that they are leaving and they never go. And you see her a few days later with another lover.

And now, in the late fall, our little romance has become a reflection. I can see her in my mind in the way I saw her first – her image, which with time has grown even stronger than it had been in reality, in the way that time and nostalgia holds on to good times. In April, in her presence, I had no will of my own and would have gone in any direction to please her. Later the experience was worth less than what I thought it would be, the illusions of youth having overruled the truth for a while. But, as autumn passed, these recollections too begin to fade, perhaps because it is no longer new and there is no mystery left in it. And I closed the book on Catherine Gray, gave up the bone for the ghost, knowing I have a higher road in which to travel, a way of my own making.

Father approaches the field and beckons us to an area near the line fence.

"We'll make the fire here, in the lee of the trees," he says. "The carry from all corners will be shorter and it is safe from sparks that could blow into the dead grass."

The stalk piles are like beaver lodges, so many alike, stationed at intervals, the best soil having been shaken from the tangled roots that reveal their productive value, enhanced by the quality of the loam, the bottom land beneath them. They are a bonus crop: fuel for a bonfire that celebrates the end of the harvest season.

Father lights a bunch on the leaf end and places it against a rock for support. The invisible flame eats through the leaves and sparks into the heavier limbs, and I ease down a sample forkful of wind-dried potato stalks and wait for them to ignite. A rope of amber smoke carries into the evening air and they burst into flame, sending sparks and curling bits of ash, cinders, and perfume well above the treetops at fireside, forming a reflection that lights up the entire field, like one would light a single room in a house.

We carry forkfuls to the fire, as orange fangs of flame, snapping and crackling because of the approaching storm, leap with a rumble into the darkness. A brown haze forms a cocoon over our little community, its fragrance colouring the sky. From the draught, the trees at fireside became a wall of multi-coloured, moving foliage that rustles in the breeze, dropping the last leaves to the already littered earth.

A screen door slams at a neighbour's farmhouse and more children scramble from their dooryards toward us, shouting and putting on their coats as they run. They would be inspired, no doubt, first by the aroma of the smoke, and then by reflections of a flame that blinks upon wallpaper and brings country folks to their windows. Upon their arriving, they say nothing, but go to the nearest stalk piles to help carry to the fire, as if to make up for the part of the evening they have missed, when lured from their supper table by shadowy figures, huddled in the distance around a fire that casts its reflections upon the harrowed earth, excitement against the melancholy of a damp autumn night. It had been an image they could not have resisted. In the words of Thomas Hardy, "Why build a bonfire if there are no children to please?"

But now, just as suddenly, I find that the neighbouring children are gone, leaving unnoticed and quietly, as if bored with a thing that has just gotten started – that, or the distant lure of the flame in reflection has been worth more than the stalk burn itself. They had not laboured in the fields, not seen the produce grow, not emptied them in the bins, and so to them the stalks meant nothing more than brush with which to build a fire.

Looking around, I can see that the stalks, in fact, have all been burned and now the fire is nothing more than a breathing dome of spark and ash that glows when the breeze blows across it. On our way to the farmhouse, I glance back at the fire site. There is one last straw blazing in the distance, and its tiny glow is filling the field with a lingering odour. This is a lasting flame, like the one that burns for a long-lost love. Finally, it twinkles in the distance and goes out.

THE STOREKEEPER

CHUCK WENT INTO THE LAUNDRYROOM THAT HAD BEEN a farmhouse pantry in former times and, looking into the mirror, put on a necktie and smoothed out his shirt collar. He was singing the Robert Goulet song "Come Saturday Morning" and his voice strained to reach the baritone levels. In the cool August morning, his wife Anne and son Stevie were still in their beds. Grabbing his sports jacket, Chuck went out the door, got into his car, and drove down the highway toward Bradford where he would spend another day in the furniture store. As he cruised along with the windows partially down, birds chirped in the trees and the fragrance of river filtered into the vehicle. He turned the radio on, and then turned it off, the better sounds coming from the countryside.

As he approached the township, there was a strong smell of sawdust from the mountains of wood chips that stood near the paper mill where many of the river people worked. And there were exhaust fumes from vehicles that crowded into the lane in front of him. Between buildings, he could glimpse the sparkle of the bay as he parked behind the store that faced the elm-treed Commons Park. He got out and, popping a match with his thumb, lit a cigarette. The cigarette slanted across his jaw, its smoke making him squint. The sun's rays were already strong as they reflected off the window glass and cement sidewalk. Making his way to the side door, he used his key to let himself inside.

The showroom smelled of new upholstery and there was the strong aroma of maple and cherry cabinetry. On the second floor where the bedroom furniture stood, there was the scent of cedar chests, and a tar-like aroma that came from the displays of floor-covering. Butting his cigarette in a sand-filled smoker, he loosened his tie and went to polish the floors. The rotary polisher howled like an electric lawnmower.

George Tanner, the store manager, who had been in the establishment since 7:30 a.m., had already put lawnmowers, tillers, and boys' wagons out onto the front sidewalk where they were locked to a parking metre with a chrome chain. Each item had a red SALE tag hanging from its handle. The store would open for business at nine o'clock sharp.

As Chuck worked the polisher, George strode about, clutching a handful of sales slips. He was singing, "*Sweet vi-o-lets, sweeter than the roooses*" and then shouting instructions to other employees. Chuck knew the furniture business was George's calling. He was a man who enjoyed the responsibility of getting the deliverymen to load the truck with the merchandise, all in the proper order for the homes along the river roads that would take most of the day to get to. The rural people were grateful to be able to buy something on the instalment plan and have it delivered to their houses so far from town. They looked upon George, not as a sales manager, but a saviour and this made him feel important. (For a time he thought about going into politics.) And in the mornings too, having spent the night in town, there were travelling sales representatives, with briefcases, who stood around the showroom waiting to be taken to the second-floor office and given an order for furniture that would not arrive from Madawaska, New Brunswick, or Bass River, Nova Scotia, for two or three months.

"I got two orders," a sales rep said to Chuck when he came down the stairs. "George told me to get out and not come back."

And there were the early morning, straw-hatted farmers who wanted to buy a lawn mower or a garden tiller before the store opened. There were also angry customers who complained about something they had bought months before. It took a diplomat to handle them. Because if one of them had a falling-out with the salesperson involved, a circle of relatives would stop dealing with him or her and no one could afford to lose that business, not in a small town like Bradford.

Chuck put these things out of his mind and went to stand near the front door. Passersby sometimes mistook him for a window mannequin, as he watched the street for a possible customer to come in, with the intentions of buying something of some worth. It would be a long hot day in the old brick store – a day of suffering from furniture polish and the floor covering smells, the heat from the big windows, without awnings, the showroom without air-conditioning; a day of trying to earn a few pennies to put toward his dream: renovation of the old tree-shaded farmhouse in Smith Falls.

In mid-afternoon, Chuck glanced out the window to see Megan Thomas and her mother Margaret walking down the sidewalk toward the store. At first he could not believe what he was seeing. His heart fluttered and for a moment his chest tightened and he was short of breath. He coughed, loosened his tie, and paced in a circle while trying to clear his throat. He was hoping his first love would not come through the door and ask him to serve her. At the thought of this, he sweated like a tray of homemade butter. To her and her folks he did not want to be identified, either as a farmer from up in Falconer – as he used to be – or a retail salesclerk who had moved downriver to Smith Falls. He had had visions of her, home on holidays, dropping in to the house to say hello, and being impressed with what he had done to the old Miller place. He was not in the right state of mind to greet her, face to face, not here, not now. He had not seen her since the breakup and always knew that meeting her again would be an emotional experience.

The Thomas women were dressed in white sundresses and sandals. Megan was wearing a big straw hat, its brim bent down in front and with a ribbon trailing down her bare back. Chuck's heartbeat quickened as he relived the times he had walked with her hand-in-hand in the fields of Smith Falls or sat beside her in the restaurants here in Bradford. This was followed by the sadness of losing her; how he tried to bury the hurt, dug it up and buried it again, and how this rejection had changed his direction in life. For a moment he resented her. Plus there was the guilt he felt after he had been with her in dreams, while sleeping with Anne. After one of those dreams, he had actually made love to Anne, with closed eyes, pretending she was Megan. It seemed like everything he did since the breakup was to make an impression on Megan – prove to her that she was wrong about him and that he could rise above what she thought was his true potential.

Not taking his eyes off the approaching women, he chewed his fingernails. His head was spinning and the pounding in his chest filled the store to make the walls pulsate. He looked at his reflection in a mirror: shabbily dressed, tie loose, hair uncombed, a cigarette stub in his hand. Oh God, he thought, I hope they walk on down the street. I don't want to be seen working here. I know she has married a professor from Ripton, Vermont.

He thought about hiding behind a tall wing chair, but looking about, saw that he was the only salesperson in the showroom. "If they come in I will have to serve them," he said out loud. "God! Spare me."

For steadiness, he grasped the back of the tall chair and tried to think of other things, even as the door opened and the women walked in. To keep his hands from shaking, he hung onto the dusty rose velour fabric. He forced himself to breathe deeply, so he could say a professional, "Good afternoon, ladies. May I serve you?" But instead he stammered, "Megan! Megan, my Megan, how have you been? Have I ever missed you! You look really great!"

He threw his arms around her like he did on the night they parted, the night he told her there would never be anyone else "no matter what happens or how old I get." And for a moment the same hurt raced through his mind. For a split second he felt sorry for himself – sorry that he could not change from who he was, then or now. It was like he and Megan had not been separated for more than an hour. And already, as before, he was trying to cover

the little man he used to be as if an apology was necessary for him
not having disappeared from the face of the earth. He realized at
once that his life's ambition had not been about restoring the old
farmhouse in Smith Falls. That it had been only a means to an end,
a way in which to impress this woman, show her that he had matured beyond the little person he used to be.

"Oh, it's Chuck. Chuck Campbell. Look, Mom, it's Chuck.
Do you remember him from … from upriver?" And then to Chuck,
"At first I didn't know you with the moustache."

There was nervous laughter, which relieved some of the
tension.

"I'm so glad you guys … dropped in!"

Chuck hugged her for a long time, until, when a shoulder replaced a breast, he sensed the embrace was being instigated by him
alone. So he let Megan go and turned and hugged her mother, a
square-jawed, no-nonsense woman who never had an ounce of use
for him.

"I'd know his hide if I saw it in a tannery," Mrs. Thomas
said. "All the upriver people look alike to me."

Those words cut like a knife.

"Mom?" Megan sounded appalled by her mother's rudeness.

"What brings you ladies to town on this hot day?"

"We're looking for floor covering for my sunroom,"
Mrs. Thomas said.

These were the words that Chuck did not want to hear. Not
floor covering, not in this heat, not something that would have him
sprawling on his knees, measuring, cutting, trying to keep the edges straight and his hands steady while struggling to keep a shred of
dignity.

"Yes, we have it. Step this way. We are short-handed today,
so I'll look after you myself. Plus I want to see that you get a good
deal." When Chuck said this, he looked over his shoulder to make
sure that George did not hear him.

He led the women up the stairs to where the scent of oilcloth and tile cement dominated; the air was stuffy and lukewarm.

Walking beside the big heavy rolls – they stood on their ends – that had gone soft from the heat, he explained the different qualities and prices per square yard: linoleum, congoleum and rex-oleum, the patterns plain, flowered, and with the black and white squares like you see in diners. He was afraid the scent of the floor covering would set off his allergies, drive him into a fit of sneezing. He could see this happening if the sale took very long.

He sneezed and wiped his nose with a pocket handkerchief. "Excuse me."

When Mrs. Thomas picked out a pattern and gave Chuck the measurements, he laid his sports jacket on a chair. Cradling the big roll, which was heavy in his arms, he strained to ease it down on the floor, quantify the size with a liberal measure. Through this, one of his penny loafers slipped off and he had to stand on one leg to put it on. And there was a hole in the toe of his sock. His face burned as he got down on his knees and used a steel straight-edge and knife to sheer the fabric. He almost cut off the end of his necktie, which made the women laugh.

"It never rains but it pours," he said. "This has turned into quite a circus!"

Beneath the smell of linoleum, Chuck could scent the sweat that dripped from his armpits to stain his shirt. And there were beads of perspiration dripping off his nose. The more he thought of his predicament, the more he perspired. He tried to think of something else, but it was impossible.

"There we go," he said finally and laboured to stand the heavy roll upright, breaking wind in the process, covering it with a cough. He hoped George would not come along and ask him to cut flooring already sold and tagged for other customers, which sometimes happened. Certainly, he did not want to be looked upon as simply the oilcloth-cutting man.

Megan sat on a chair, her tanned legs crossed at the knees, thong sandal dangling from a big toe. Her sunglasses twirled in her right hand.

Chuck looked at her pretty legs below the skirt and a flicker of grief flashed through his mind. He could feel she was looking at his not-so-pretty persona and perhaps with a sense of witticism, which also added to his humiliation. And he wondered if she felt anything, either now or in the past, toward him. Because she acted as if he were just another sales clerk she might stumble upon in any department store, as if he had come from a previous life she had no memory of. Women are loved more when they become more elusive, he thought, and for a second, wondered if she had ever been what he thought she was. He figured that the kind of women who attracted him were above him socially and stayed with him only until someone more compatible came along.

And he wondered what it was about *him* that had attracted her back then. Had he been the only eligible teenager in the community? For a moment he wished she would die so he could put her out of his mind, put her memory to rest and go on with his humble life, perhaps even melt back into the upriver scene. Falconer would be okay if she was dead. There would be no reason to leave that lazy, carefree lifestyle with her gone. But instantly he felt ashamed for thinking along these lines because, for a few months, back then, she had given him the happiest moments of his life. And even in the rejection of him, especially in the rejection of him, her denial had inspired him to reach higher. He watched her, watching him as he rolled up the square and bound it with twine.

He wanted to ask her why she had strung him along until September before dropping the bomb. Did she know this was going to happen even while they were sharing those wonderful moments? Was there anything more he could have done to make things work? Or had Vermont been in the picture even then? He wanted to ask her if she remembered the night after her graduation when they had gone to Point Cheval Beach, the sex, the words spoken so passionately. But of course he could not ask her any of these things. And it saddened him to think that such emotions, such important memories, could not be revisited even while he was bursting at the seams, trying to contain a love that, in her absence, had grown stronger if anything. And he wondered if she would even remember the events that had been so engrained and would stay in his own mind forever. He could feel his face flush as he carried the sewer-pipe-size roll of flooring down the stairs, nervously wrote up a sales slip, and the office woman made the change for Mrs. Thomas.

"Now sharpen your pencil," Margaret had said. "I'm expecting a good deal from this fellow."

Chuck carried the floor covering out the front door and down the sidewalk to the Thomas station wagon where he slid it in the back window, realizing it would take more than a sport's jacket or necktie to elevate him from the working class.

Before they got into the car, Mrs. Thomas said, "Was it you who bought the old Miller house up home?"

"Yes, I moved back from Toronto last spring." Chuck said these words to Mrs. Thomas, but they were meant for Megan's ears.

"It's a big old barracks of a place that will be costly to heat." She turned and looked at Chuck for the first time that day.

"Yes, it is big, but not without a purpose. I have plans to make it into a country inn," Chuck said and laughed. "I guess I'm a romantic."

"What a great idea," Megan said. "Vermont has many inns."

"Did you marry someone from upriver then?" Mrs. Thomas tilted her head forward to look over her glasses.

"No, no, my wife comes from Stony Creek, Ontario. She's an actress. We met at the Shakespeare Festival in Stratford." He glanced toward Megan, who was again gazing at the Commons Park.

"Well, I can see that you have made some improvements in the old place already. Of course it was unsightly before."

"Mom?"

Mrs. Thomas smiled and did not say anything more. But Chuck thought, What arrogance comes with a little money.

"Well, good luck with it," Megan said and brushed him with a half, sidelong hug.

He wanted to ask if she would meet him later that evening, in the back fields of Smith Falls where they could fall together by chance and he could unburden some of his long-suffered grief. But of course he could not do that.

The women got into the car – with the Vermont licence plates – and drove away, leaving Chuck standing on the sidewalk. In the store's window, he could see his reflection; he appeared to be short and tilted off-kilter from defeat. She has put me through the meat grinder again, he thought. And he laughed out loud at the awkwardness, the bad timing of the moment. He danced and he laughed and then with his head down, he leaned against the building and cried, because he found there was not much difference between these emotions.

He wondered how, when he got home, he was going to keep these feelings hidden from Anne and not show a dark mood swing that would be hard to explain. After supper, he would take a long walk in the fields where the natural images were always enshrouded with the spirit of old memories. And which he knew would bring her back in the old-fashioned sense, and he would keep her there in that place. He thought, We sometimes refuse to change in our dreams, even as we try to change in our hearts. But the mind is not the heart, and wise people, like Megan, follow the mind. While one's heart clings to a glorified past, in stages, the other's mind is changing, moving forward, so that through time the connection of the two becomes more remote. Our old selves are no longer with us in anything we do; such is the realness of maturing.

That night he dreamt of Megan; in the dream, it was the morning after her graduation. He had awakened to see her beside him in bed, reached and turned her over to kiss her lips and eyes, which had a creamy scent of makeup. They held one another long and deep in the kiss and made love again. When he awoke and realized where he was, he felt a thrust of sadness. This was followed by an irresistible sense of shame because he had taken refuge in Megan even as he slept. He stared at the ceiling and his love for Megan struggled with his sense of fairness toward Anne. And for a time there were three of them, with Stevie and Mrs. Thomas in the centre of the triangle. He got out of bed, went to the window, drew aside the curtain, and tried to see the Thomas house, which was beyond the tracks near the river. But with all the full-leafed trees, it was obscured from view. He thought, It is a curse for someone to be as beautiful as Megan. It is a curse to those who fall in love with them, are jilted, and carry that love inside us through life. And it's a curse to the women we marry after having loved her first. For none among us will find true happiness thereafter. And then he thought, The past is only an illusion I have dreamed up, kept alive as an escape from real life. Anne loves me and I love her. She is the real thing. I must shake this nostalgic ghost.

THE CURFEW

IN SEPTEMBER I WALK IN OUR COUNTRY CHURCHYARDS. I pause here and there to read an inscription on a gravestone as I look for the names of relatives who have gone before my time, as well as the ones that I can remember. And there are others to whom I am loosely related, their graves blooming readily with for-get-me-nots. Of course there are many people buried here who are not related to me. Some of the older ones I have heard about, their deeds or misdeeds passed down through word of mouth, having had reputations as fighters or crooks, or perhaps a more honour-able occupation such as a teacher or a doctor.

On some of those old tombstones are names – barely legible – that date back two centuries, six or seven generations. These people arrived in Canada on sailing ships, having been starved out of the old country through famine or perhaps they were sent here as remittance people of no class distinction, trou-bled souls that the aristocrats wanted to get rid of. But now, here in this graveyard, in this country, all are of the same worth and class as they sleep under similar quality stone markers, all shaded by the same, age-old elm trees. And I think that there is something about a cemetery, and time, that equalizes, brings everyone to a level playing field, to sleep in unison, side by side, through eternity.

Also buried in these wild-flowered funeral grounds are the scoundrels that I can remember having lived in my own time. Their crimes are almost forgotten and their tombstones are com-parable in a field of many. And I think that one more generation will wipe out their troubled legacy. As well, there are the less-mentioned saints: my mother, my elementary teacher, and my first love among them. Their names are literally carved in stone, their images strong in my mind – like pastoral portraits on stained glass – to be admired, because they had never sinned. They were muted Miltons, living out of the spotlight, doing good deeds for all who knew and remember them. These are the people who made our communities whole.

The younger names move me the most – my contemporaries, and their children and grandchildren. These people lay sleeping, their underdeveloped characters beneath the newly turned earth where there is not yet even a good sod. Their graves are marked with a white cross or perhaps a hockey stick, and a scattering of plastic flowers. I grieve, not for the children that are gone, but for the parents who are forced to live with the hurt, brought on more vividly as evening and winter falls. They will arise from oblivion as saints in the future generations of infinity.

Sometimes I see the images of these special people: the teacher, the loved ones, the individuals who made a difference in *my* life. They appear as portraits in the framed windows of their now abandoned farmhouses when the setting sun reflects through the cracks in the closed-up shutters to make a stairway of golden steps. And I think of it as their ladder to the great beyond. They will never lose their eloquence because of obscurity, not in my time. Indeed, if grave markers or derelict houses could speak, there would be an epic novel in each of them.

I approach a headstone that has an open book and a music symbol engraved over the name, Mrs. Caroline Henley 1921-2001. And I think of this marvelous woman as a teacher in our little one-room school, a mentor to all who knew her, a mother of ten daughters, a housewife, an accomplished pianist, and a pillar of our community.

Having come from a well-to-do family in the city of Fredericton, Caroline Henderson arrived in our community to teach school in the fall of 1940. She was fresh out of Normal School.

Caroline found a boarding house – the old Armstrong place – and settled in to do her work, walking a mile to school in the early mornings, and trodding back under the purple skies of evening. She was a tall, willowy, blonde-haired woman, with blue eyes, square white teeth, and freckles on her nose. When I was in grade four I was in love with her.

Everyone said that Caroline Henderson had knowledge, education, and culture and was a great influence on anyone who knew her. The young men in our community had an interest in the good-looking teacher and one in particular, Jack Henley – he had a little smattering of education himself but was quite a lot older – visited her often, taking her for long walks in the Anderson fields and woods, and down by the river, eventually asking her to marry him.

Jack Henley was a small man from a rundown property a mile upriver from home and, on the other side, a farmstead that had never prospered, even in the best of times. Around the old Henley house on the hilltop, the broad fields extended for many acres to the distant woods where rail fences kept back the pressing trees. Midway across those fields was an old gray barn that was saddled-backed, with sunken doors that led onto a threshing floor, and a cow's stable with two cows and a bull that was haltered under the straw-covered scaffold.

People on that side of the river said our farm was so fallow that at haying time you would have to drive stakes in the ground to see where the mowing machine had gone. And the people on our side said the only thing that anyone could raise over on the Henley farm was a disturbance. But Jack Henley's property had a big intervale down by the river where the low meadow land was richer because of it having been flooded in the spring freshets and that was where the vegetables were planted. When I was still yet a boy, on hot summer days, I would sometimes walk upriver along our shore to where I could see Jack, Caroline, and some of the older daughters, on their knees, weeding the garden. Each one took a drill and worked their way up the hill. And when this work was done, the girls ran to the river where they swam and capered and there was a lot of screeching and laughter.

On the hillside in front of the gray, shingled farmhouse, there were huge elm trees and the river could be seen as it made a horseshoe that stretched for two miles in each direction. From their spooled veranda, it was a spectacular view – especially on spring mornings when the sun was at your back and the shadows of the elm stretched toward the sparkling water, the blue hills beyond. And there was the scent of hawthorn blossom around the bevelled-glass front door. But inside, the house was shabby with the open, hand-hewn beams, plank floors, and, up a set of stairs, the small, slanted-ceiling bedrooms that had dormers facing the river. Like my home, there was no indoor plumbing and the place was heated by a small wood-burning kitchen range and in the main house, a decorative parlour stove. Caroline was well past her child-bearing years before the hydropower and a telephone were installed. But this was where she had conceived, given birth to, and raised her large family.

Jack Henley was a slow-moving man who at farming time walked behind his slow-walking horses. And in winter he sat on bobsleds as his team hauled pulpwood across the river ice to the boxcars that were on the railway switch a half-mile down the highway from our place. Jack always seemed to have the same slow pace – as did my father – and his horses had taken on his personality, as horses will, and appeared to be sleepwalking.

Sometimes, on winter nights, when the girls and their mother were doing homework, Jack made his way across the river, where the moonlight reflected his thin shadow upon the blue snow, on into the darkness of the bank trees, feeling his way for the glass footprints that were closer together on the hill as he manoeuvred his way down the path to my father's store. He wore a mackinaw coat and under a stocking-leg cap his hair was white, like snow that gathers on the heads of park statues. In the store, he sat by the stove with a half-dozen fiddle-backed old men, my father among them, telling yarns and playing cards. And to me, even at my young age, these men appeared uninteresting, as opposed to Mrs. Henley, where in school her very presence revealed not vice but virtue. Jack never was in any hurry to leave, even at closing time.

Caroline was always busy with schoolwork and a young family that was growing with each year. Many of her babies were born in the dead of winter, a time when a doctor had to travel twenty miles over blustery roads, change his boots and winter coats in our store, and, with a horse lantern, venture up the flat and across the river ice, following the little bushes that marked a safe passage, to where he waited for another baby to arrive. Caroline raised ten children, all of whom were tall, blue-eyed, blonde-haired women with their mother's demeanour; all were scholarly and, like their mother, had an interest in literature and music.

Once in a while Caroline's father, who was a merchant in the capital city, came to visit his daughter and granddaughters. He got off the train at the siding stop near home and walked across the ice with boxes that contained some of the fashions of the day. Occasionally during holidays, Caroline took the train to visit her folks. In the morning, alone, she flagged down The Express, and during the two-hour journey through open farm country, with a dozen siding stops along the way, she was not even cognisant of the ongoing habitual scenery: the spirit of the old gray barns with a few scattered snowflakes in the wind, the melancholy clapboard farmhouses, the corn land with its visible yellow stubble, the purple woods on the distant hills.

Instead she worked on her school assignments. With a red pencil, she corrected examination papers and essays; her focus on the written word, and the unworthy children of letters who attended her classroom. Years later, as an adult, took my life in that direction, her influence having inspired my love for literature and music.

And how often I thought since, that in the people we love and are mentored by, there is an ambition, a dream which we cannot really comprehend at the time, but which we unconsciously pursue, because they are heartfelt goals, inspired by mature soul people.

In the city, Caroline shopped in the big department stores, before boarding the train at the York Street Station to head back home, arriving in our community near midnight. After hearing the squeal of the train's wheels in the downgrade, I would arise from my bed to see Mrs. Henley walking past, a scarf wrapped around her face, her arms filled with shopping bags. On those hollow winter nights, I could hear the crunching of her overshoes in the dry snow. After one of those trips away, all the Henley girls came to school wearing stylish new caps and dresses.

When the winter was mostly over, the ice had left the river, and the trout and black salmon were running, I could see the Henley daughters on the other side, where they stood at the water's edge, casting fishing lines out into the big moving river, which was deeper along that shore because it was in the bend. They took home much needed strings of trout and sometimes a grilse for their mother to fry. The fish appeared bigger in April, especially from their side, and were easier to catch too. At such times the girls bantered over the best places in which to stand, taking turns in the hot spots at the mouth of the brook. For it was a feather in one's caps to bring home fish. They also built grass fires and burned off the riverbanks along with the driftwood and dead shore grass the flood waters had left on the flats.

I remember a morning in April when an old river guide who used to sometimes take me fishing stopped his boat at the Henley shore and offered to take three of the older girls for a ride. They did not know this man was drinking alcohol, and, unseen by their mother, and for excitement, they got into the boat and went with him. When at mid-stream he started to do manoeuvres, spinning the craft in small circles and bouncing back over the cross-chop, the boat capsized. The girls had to swim to safety, which was a great task in water that was just two or three degrees above freezing. The old guide clung to his boat and eventually got to shore. It was a great lesson for the young women to be wary of people who had unfavourable intentions and very few brains.

Later in the summer, in the Henley backfields, the short-stemmed oats were green, with a scattering of yellow mustard weed here and there – oats that would never grow tall enough to be cut with a binder and bound into sheaves. Before dinnertime, when the sky was clear to the horizons, on the steep hillside – back of the rows of potato plants, now in blossom – the hay was cut, by hand. And I can remember hearing the scythe-stone clanging, behind the motion, its peel being delayed by the distance between me and those faraway fields, the ring changing its tone from the blade's heel to the toe.

In the afternoon in shorts and halter tops, the sunburned daughters pitched the scattered windrows into the wagon rack, some with pitchforks, some in armloads, as their father drove his horses and built the load. The younger daughters worked with the wooden rakes to gather what was left on the ground and pass it up to their father, the horses switching their tails to chase off the house- and horseflies. Later, this light hay, fine-top mostly because it was impossible to seed the hillside, was pitched off by hand into the mows and scaffolds of the barns, and stowed away by the daughters. It was obvious that Jack Henley loved his farm and the hard life he had been born into, and so wanted for nothing more. I used to think he was the most contented man I ever knew and his farm and family were his world.

After a day in the fields – as we all did in the country, because of the lack of indoor plumbing – the girls ran to the river where they frolicked and swam in circles around one another, screeching and diving deep, to resurface a long way out. And I wished that I had been a swimmer.

As the daughters grew and matured, sometimes they came to our store to have ice cream or a Coke. And the young lads who hung around the shop walked them home. But the Henleys had no interest in the local boys who they had watched stumble through the school lessons, perhaps not having given full play to their faculties in the fear of appearing effeminate. They were people who had no dreams and lived only for the day's pleasure. On their mother's advice, the girls would better themselves and their family by marrying more ambitious men from away, beyond that hard-luck farm country. For a time, I had an interest in one of them, and sometimes we walked together from the school to my place, but of course the regional frame of mind was deeply ingrained in me and with no comprehensible future in sight, I knew better than to try to woo her. Every so often the Henley girls came to our house to sing while my brother Jack played the piano. And they entered their names in the talent contests that took place in the village.

Caroline herself had been an accomplished pianist, having grown up in the city where music lessons were the norm. But she had to give up her music when she married Jack as in the Henley farmhouse there was no money or interest in something as frivolous as classical music. Once or twice a year, Caroline came to our house with a valise filled with sheet music and she played our piano. And I can remember the beautiful music she made, Chopin and Beethoven in all the different flats and sharps. Her neat musical phrasing – as in my mother's embroidery, the blue violets in the wallpaper, and over the mantle, a portrait of King George VI – spun a tapestry of former times, a romantic old day that was filled with tranquility and elegance.

One evening, just before suppertime and not long after her mother died, Caroline came to our house and played Chopin's *Sonata Number Two in B flat minor* – blinking to hold back her tears – which awakened new feelings of melancholy inside me. It was a funeral piece for sure and I considered myself lucky to have been moved by her music thus. Until Mum asked me to leave the room so that Mrs. Henley could be at one with her music and her thoughts. I recall sitting on the grass just under the screened living room window, in the shade of a birch tree, and above the hum of insects, listened to her refined melancholy air. Once, to hear her play, I stood silently behind the living room door. Mrs. Henley was an instrumentalist and not a great singer, as I recall from the schoolroom when she led us through "O Canada" and "God Save the Queen," her homely air making her more motherly than disciplined. And during those long winter evenings at home, I thought of her, without a piano, and how unfair it was.

It was a long walk from the Henley farmhouse to our one-room school, which was a mile down the gravel roadstead from my home. But Caroline never missed a day because of bad weather. I remember scraping the frost from my bedroom window and watching for her to come down the flat on blustery mornings when the temperature was minus thirty – a time when I thought perhaps there would be no school due to the nature of the day. And she would appear on the river ice, to follow the awkward little towpath, leading her parade of daughters, with the oldest ones in front and smallest at the back: goslings behind a mother goose. And the winter-clad figures, with their long blowing scarves, puffing steam as they following the crooked row of black alders, with the slanted farmhouse and barn in the background, was a Maud Lewis painting.

I remember, too, sitting in that little three-windowed, clapboard schoolhouse, watching the snow swirl about the windows, and wondering if Mrs. Henley was going to let us go home early. But she never did. And sometimes if it was real nasty, in late afternoons, Jack Henley came to the school with his big horse and portage sled and gave everyone a ride home, dropping us off at our respective houses, where Caroline, in her high overshoes, the tails of her coat catching the wind, walked the little ones to their front doors while Jack held the horse. There was no such thing as a "snow day" back then.

In school, Mrs. Henley was fair and showed no favour to her own daughters. She made all her pupils seem special, bringing out the best in each of us. It was like she could see inside her pupils' souls, to observe what we were thinking. And she touched us in these sensitive and most closely held places. This made us all try harder because we wanted to please *her*. When she stood at the front of the class, with her spectacles on the bridge of

her nose, and read from the old school readers – *Up and Away,
All Sails Set,* or *Life and Adventure* – she brought the scenes and
the characters to life, as she did with the poetry of Alfred Noyes
("The Highwayman"), Wilfred Campbell ("Indian Summer"), or
E. Pauline Johnson ("The Song of My Paddle.")

As Mrs. Henley read, she walked back and forth in front
of the blackboard, smoothing out the leaves of the book with the
palm of her left hand, putting emphasis on the most important
phrases, and lifting her eyes to look at the class only when she finished a sentence, an index finger marking the page. (Sometimes she
read a couple of lines of poetry and asked us who the author was,
on occasion tricking us with a fragment of poetry that one of the
older students – possibly one of her daughters – had written. And
she would glance at me with a glad eye if I detected her prank.)
I have listened to many readers in my time, but I have never
heard anyone – the quality of the prose not withstanding – bring
the written word to life like Mrs. Henley. It was always a pleasure
to listen to her read, either to my class or the ones in the higher
grades.

And when she asked me to write an essay on this or that
subject, she would have me read it aloud to the class, saying,
"This boy has taken pains." Once I stood by my desk and nervously read an essay I had written about the woodpeckers I had
encountered while working in the woods with my father during
the Christmas holidays. And in reading my little composition, the
words brought back the sting of the northeast wind, the blind-
ing snow squalls, the scent of our lunch fire as we drank tea in
the woods, and of course my bedroom study – Mother had set
up a card table with a chair and a lamp as a place for me to do
my homework, as I had asthma in those days and missed a lot of
school time – which had so much of Mum's soul in it. In the essay
I had used the phrases "at length" and "after which." (*I stood watching a red headed woodpecker and at length it flew into a tall tree,
after which it disappeared completely. Sadly, I never saw or heard that
pretty little bird again.*) Of course, I was using the words I had read

in my grade six textbook. Or perhaps I had heard Mrs. Henley read them. And I know if I were to read that article even now, however vivid my recollections of the past may be, for a moment I would be that little boy again, and in that wood.

"Good, but just a tad sentimental," she said. "Did anyone else notice?"

She rolled a pencil between her hands to make a click when it passed her wedding ring while she told us how not to be sad in our essays and that sentimentality was not a virtue but a flaw in storytelling.

"But aren't we supposed to write what we feel, like we do in poetry?" I asked.

"Yes, but in prose we need a vision that can move the reader, plus a technique that will make the story evolve without too much sentiment."

Sometimes, she asked me to go to the shed to fetch some firewood for the big sow-bellied stove that stood near her desk. And she knelt on one knee and lifted the split maple blocks into the fire through the cast-iron open door – the blinking fire giving her face a copper tint, her round glasses Ghandi-like.

While she described Christmas as an "uproar" for parents, she always put on a great Examination Day Concert with all of us taking part in recitations, dialogues, and singing, as we did at the Junior Red Cross meetings on Friday afternoons.

Once on a Friday afternoon, Mrs. Henley's daughter Helen and I were throwing paper missiles that contained a message across the classroom to one another. When one that I threw curved and landed at Mrs. Henley's feet, she picked it up and read, "I think that you have the nicest bum in the school!" I watched her face turn pale and then red, her mouth tighten. "I know this boy's handwriting and I am vexed!" she said. "I want him to stay in the classroom at recess." Of course I played innocent. But when at recess I stood to file out with the others, she caught my arm as I walked past. "I think the boy who threw the note knows who I am speaking to," she said. It was then that her daughter spoke up to say the note was meant for her and that she had thrown similar messages to me. We were given a lecture but were spared the strap, which was the ultimate punishment at the time. Afterwards, I could never recall that incident without a feeling of guilt and shame.

One winter when I was still in my early teens – I had gotten through grade eight and against my mother's wishes had quit school – I worked with Jack Henley in his woods. We were cutting pulpwood in two feet of snow in a valley, back on the banks of McCord Brook. I dressed warm and left home at daybreak, walking across the river ice and up that big hill on what seemed like a dog path, drifted over. The sky was gray like the steel of old axes, and there was six inches of new snow covering the unused sill of the Henley's bevelled-glass front door. Jack was in the barn, but in their little kitchen, Caroline and her daughters were crowded around the wood range, eating buckwheat porridge from bowls and bantering over pieces of clothing – warm scarves and stockings to keep them from catching cold – as they made preparations to head out on that long trek to school.

After a few words about the weather, Mrs. Henley said that she wished I would go back to school and not rely on woods-work for a livelihood. "You deserve better," she said.

This was a little message that I took to heart.

Through time, Caroline's daughters, one by one, went off to boarding schools in town where they received their high school education. Then they moved away and married, as was Mrs. Henley's wish. And when Jack Henley, broken down from the years of hard work, died of pneumonia in the winter of '72, the farmhouse was closed up and later sold for its water frontage and fishing privileges. Mrs. Henley got an apartment – with a piano – in her home city and I had not heard much from her for a long time. I knew that some of her daughters had died young, and I wrote to her on these occasions. But I can remember walking up along our riverbank and looking across the river to where the post-sunset inflamed the windows of the Henley farmhouse, long since abandoned. And I knew that if I listened carefully, I could hear the scamper of feet, the rattle of pots on the cook stove, the slamming of doors, as Caroline and her daughters set out for their morning trek to school, which by then had also been closed down due to regional consolidation. Such was the fate of those northeast farm communities.

But then one afternoon, in August of '01, I was on my way to work as a salmon guide on the river when I noticed a number of cars parked along the road in front of the United Church near home. When I stopped and asked a local man whose funeral it was, he told me that it was Mrs. Caroline Henley. Though rushed for time, and dressed in work clothes, I found my way inside and sat in the nave of the old country church. The daughters and their husbands were there, middle-aged people by this time. And there were a number of grandchildren who at first glance appeared to have some of their grandmother's demeanour. As the service went on, I wept to think that as a boy I had felt a great affection for this woman, and now admired her as a mentor – an ambitious and philosophical mother and educator. I listened to the hymn singing – "Praise Him! Praise Him!" – and the prayers – "*O grave, where is thy Victory?*" – and I must admit that my recollections took over the service and carried me along.

But during the eulogy, the minster mentioned that I had been one of her favourite pupils, and read a passage from a book I had written many years before; something about how we keep a person alive inside ourselves through memory, and how we carry their presence and habits with us to our own graves, even though their origins may be long since forgotten. "Something of a person lives on after death," he read. "Having placed ourselves into the psyche of our mentor's work ethic and art, it is unconsciously passed down to the next generation."

And I was pleased to think that we had not grown apart philosophically, that even in death, Caroline Henley was encouraging me to keep working on what she knew was my life's passion, the written word.

Years later when I ventured over to the old Henley place on a Thanksgiving Sunday, I found that without its people, the abandoned farm had no soul, and it took on the appearance of a wasteland. There was barely a trace of the house's rock foundation. But there was a squeaky water pump with its long arm flung high, as if in defeat, a stack of used bricks from the chimney, and in the trees under a lattice of branches, the iron wheels of a rusty raking machine – all made more mournful by the squawk of a raven – which at once conjured up the spirit of Jack Henley. These things and the old apple tree were all that was left standing to bear the place's name.

Of course Caroline had never been suited to the Henley place anyway – her daughters were her passion and her perish – and through time, hardship has a way of being wiped out of one's past. My strongest memories of her come now from our living room where she played my mother's piano, this and the wonderful school readings. But I also can see her in the waltzes of Chopin, the sonatas of Beethoven. I find her in the poetry of E. Pauline Johnson and Wilfred Campbell. Her image appears on the grounds where our little schoolhouse used to stand and on the playground where, as a boy, I rambled at recess, trying to memorize a poem, just for her. And I glimpse a faint likeness in her granddaughters who are now teachers in the city. Indeed, Caroline Henley has left a legacy and was a forerunner to the modern-day woman.

When a person like Caroline Henley dies, they immediately become saints in the minds of those of us who loved and were mentored by them. But to everyone else, she would be just another headstone, equal to all the others, in a little country churchyard.

PREVAILING WINDS

ON THE LAST EVENING OF OCTOBER, MARK PUT ON HIS
pea jacket and, with a sea captain's cap low on his brow, went
with his son to visit the neighbours. It was just before dusk, the
sky clear, and there was a giant moon that coppered the east-
ern horizon, turning the sun-baked fields into shades of orange.
Flocking birds sat on power lines like ducks in a pinball machine.
And a breeze which carried the smell of sawdust – for Mark, images of cutting stove wood as a boy with his father – conveyed a
sharp winter chill as it swept over the fences and the hawthorn-
treed lane. It felt not exactly like a night of approaching rain;
rather the sharpness in the wind was striving to make it a night
of approaching rain, or snow, the shadows and black windows in
harmony with the season of All Hallows' Eve. A carved pumpkin,
lighted with a homemade candle, sat upon a limb in a garden oak.
With the tree bare of leaves, the jack-o-lantern could be seen
throughout the community of Blueberry Ridge. It twinkled like a
medieval mask. And there was the scent of ashes from where in the
yard leaves had burned the evening before.

This was the only night of the year that Mark visited his
neighbours and he looked forward to it. Hearing his knock, they
came to their lighted front doors and greeted him with handshakes,
while inviting him and his son Nathaniel into the over-warmth of
their wood-heated kitchens. Mark carried a flask of brandy, and as
his son held out his plastic pumpkin to receive treats of homemade
fudge, his father offered the householders a taste of *his* spirits.

They chatted excitedly as they drank from snifters.

At the Bell house they were invited into the parlour – so Georgian – for apples and oranges. Mrs. Bell, a retired nurse, made a big to-do about trying to guess who the child was, as if she had not seen them leaving home to take a shortcut across the fields to her back door. "Now who would this be with the scary mask?" she asked, winking at Mark while offering Nathaniel a hug. "Oh my soul, you frightened me." Nathaniel told her he was five and a half years old.

Mark treated Mrs. Bell to a drink before moving on. As they walked along the broken sidewalk, Mark thought, It is good to get out of the house. It is good to walk with my son, mingle with the neighbours once in a while. Someday, I will be a pillar in this community. It is also comforting to be in my own space for a time. He thought, I'm putting on the dog a bit tonight. Maybe it's because of the brandy. Or maybe Halloween is the time to open up, reveal one's true character. I love this old village, he thought. There is beauty in all things here.

At the Anderson House, the largest and most elegant in the community, they walked along the spooled veranda while wondering which door they should knock on. And an old woman who lived in The Plaza Hotel in New York City, but who summered here because it had been her home, came to the side door and apologized because she had no treats for the child, saying she had completely forgotten what night it was. Still, Mrs. Anderson invited them into her kitchen, had a brandy with Mark, lit a cigarette, and asked him to sit a while and fill her in on all the news.

"Are you the young man who activated the old Robertson place?"

"Yes, I love that house. My wife and I are going to fix it up. I hope."

"I think that is a marvellous idea. It's a wonderful old home that used to be a rooming house, and with such beautiful trees. When I was a girl I stayed there a lot with Anne and Susan Robertson. We went to school together, you know. God bless them, they are both gone now. Well, I hope it works out for you. So many stately old places – so hard to heat and maintain – are being torn down. And some are being replaced with trailers and the like."

"Yes, I hope I can make it work. It's a dream I've had for years." And then he added, "What schools did you go to?"

"The Blueberry Ridge Elementary, of course, and then to private schools in different places. I went to the Rothesay Collegiate and then on to Harvard."

"What a wonderful legacy you have. Boy, there were great families living in Blueberry Ridge in those days. When my mother was a teenager she worked down here as a chambermaid."

"Yes, many upriver girls did – hard-working, clean young women. We thought we were good families anyway. The lumber trade kept this community thriving: the mills, the great log drives, and the shipbuilding of course. But everything is different now. The times have changed."

"I know. And not for the better," Mark said. "Come along, Nathaniel."

Mark and Nathaniel moved on up the sidewalk to the next house. But Mark knew he would invite this woman and some other neighbours to drop by his place later in the fall for a cup of tea, a Sunday afternoon of chit-chat.

As they walked from door to door and other children from the community joined their throng, they referred to Mark as Captain High Liner. Sometimes a car went past and its occupants shouted, "Trick or treat, Zorba the Greek!"

Across the river, a witch's ride to the southeast, a fire was burning in the centre of a big field – perhaps the corn or potato stalks that had been left from the harvest. There were leaping orange flames, and the smoke filled the night with a sweet-scented perfume, the remote farmhouse, with its lonely window lamps, reflecting in the background. Some men stood around a deer that hung in the open doors of a barn. This reminded Mark of his early years in Falconer where on Halloween nights, he and his friends went from farm to farm upsetting outhouses. And they also burned leaves and old fence rails on the highway.

When they got back home, Pam was entertaining a group of children she had invited in, and who were bobbing for apples. They wanted her to take them into the old dark barn.

Later in the night, when the family was in their four-poster, patchwork beds, Mark was brought to a window by distant flames that blinked upon the wallpaper. It was the old and long vacated Roland place, which stood near the railway tracks and which had also been a rooming house for mill workers in former times. Its shingles having grown black from decay, the house was said to have been haunted by a headless mill worker (with a long blade) who had chased people away and so the children were not allowed to go near it, although for excitement, some of the older ones did. Now the flames were shooting out through the empty windows and doors and the burning rafters were visible like the ribs in an upside-down skeletal boat, curls of red smoke sending up among the trees, the black flood meadows beyond. It was one more symbol of the glory days of Blueberry Ridge being devoured from the landscape.

With Indian summer over, the golden autumn days had turned to gray, the weather cold and windy with spits of rain slanting up the river. Mark bundled up and, with the shotgun under his arm and the dog at his side, went for a walk in the back pastures where there were hard-baked mud trails the cows had made, and beyond the fence, a field of corn stook. In the birch grove he saw a grouse running on the leaves. He raised the gun but realized he had forgotten his cartridges. Frost, he thought. This is so much like a day he described in his great poem "My November Guest." Mark sat on a knoll, making a saddle-like imprint in the grass, and, taking a notebook from his bag, observed and wrote every detail, as real and as movingly as he could describe it.

Mark was so close to the land (so near had he been to it in former times) that when he walked, notebook in hand in these pastoral fields or wood, in any season, he would stop to observe the fleeting little scenes: a bird chirping among bare boughs, wildflowers nodding in a breeze, the scent of frost-killed bracken, the taste of rain in the air. And he relived the moments these images stirred inside him, subconscious memories from the days when he worked the land and woods with his father. Or perhaps meditations from a centuries-old poem by Blake or Wordsworth he had recently studied, the melancholy of which he would try to put into his own poetry and claim as his genius, in the way that two men might feel passion for a woman whose charm has attracted both, neither realizing that the inspiration was not his, rather the fruits of *her* persuasion which was the greater art form, the master voice. In this case it was Frost (he had also been a nature observer), and then the real landscape.

This happened especially on days that had character – mood days of freezing skies, dark winds, rain, or perhaps a brush of snow. For these walks in late autumn, Mark had bought for himself, at the Salvation Army Thrift Store, a good second-hand tweed jacket, with leather patches on the elbows, and a long plaid scarf. He walked with the old Irish setter, stopping here and there to examine perhaps an abandoned birds' nest and marvel at its structure, a wild thistle gone to seed, or a rosehip bush laden with red berries. And in the distance he would imagine the tinkle of sheep bells. These inspirations he scribbled in his notepad, a poem for the English class.

Sometimes through long periods of autumn rain or near rain, when a gale was tearing at the old farmhouse chimneys, he strolled down by the river, bucking the shoulder of the wind that tossed against the water's flow to make it look like a cornfield in a hurricane. In the short twilight of those rugged November evenings, he enjoyed being out of doors because he could smell, even taste, the land and the water that trickled along in deep ruts that the iron-soled mill wagons had made years before. The trees along the shore, with here and there a cluster of orange or yellow leaves, still clinging, were a sharp contrast to the black alders that made the scene appear like an amateur painting in progress. Such were his observations, the artistic life he craved and that appeared to be eluding him. He would stand in meditation as he looked across the Robertson Intervale to see the gables of his farmhouse with their clay chimney pots with the blue woodsmoke curling toward heaven. And he would envision a century-old inn with a dripping, thatched roof, yellow-lighted windows, and stone fence, somewhere in the marshes of literary England.

When night was falling and the only sounds were the crunch of his footsteps, or a distant church bell, more mellow than clear, he went back to his farmhouse, sat by the fire, the flames of which reflected orange against the gilt picture frames, and looked out at hailstones coming down, one by one, and tried to compose a poem out of the experience. Sometimes he would read Dickens or perhaps the naturalist W. H. Hudson, English writers who also inspired him to put pen to paper in an attempt to capture the moment. He would find music to suit the mood, something that carried in its symbols the tranquillity of centuries past, and compare his emotions to the great poet/philosophers of that time. He felt that his first-hand field observations were a great advantage, especially when analyzing the nature poets.

So when the mood day was right, he would grasp it, relive the literature-inspired scene through his own senses. He associated each image, be it materialistic or sensual, scientific or artistic, to some emotion. And he made notes, a few words he could use in a poem down the road when he had more time to write, realizing that it was easier to "observe" a scene than to write it into verse. He had started one such poem in 1965 but had never completed it, as the right words kept eluding him. Or perhaps he would use the moment for a better grade in an essay for his English class. Then he would compare his notes to feelings he got when reading a certain poem; a Frost, a Blake, or a Wordsworth day would be identified and secretly marked in his journal. Such was the preoccupation to grasp his thought potential.

The exercise helped in writing the journals about his boyhood, even though most of it came out of hardship and was painful to relive, or perhaps it was because it lay heavily on his conscience and the field meditations served as an escape, especially the sadness around his brother Timmy's death years ago, which he still blamed on himself, his brother having fallen into the wood splitter on his watch. At that time the priest had sent him to the land for meditations with God. There was always healing in the land.

At the old farmhouse in December, little half-moons of snow gathered at the bottom of window sashes and icicles hung from the eaves. A wind blew in at the bottom of the doors. There was a buildup of ice on the back step that kept the storm door from closing tightly and it was near impossible for Mark to keep the driveway free of snow so he could get to the car, which was plugged into a lamp post. (Last fall he had installed Dickens-like lamps at the different entrances, plus one at the back door and one in the garden. These he turned on with a switch from inside.) Sometimes on dark snowy days or winter evenings, the outside lamps were kept lighted so he could see the storm's intensity in reflections cast upon the ground. They brightened up the picket-fenced dooryard against the rawness of the uncultivated countryside, as did the Maple Leaf flag that flapped on a pole beside the driveway.

Northern gales whistled across the adjacent pasture and through the bare branches of the oak, the cracks in the clapboards and the poor-fitting window panes, to inflate the curtains on the windward side and turn the dormers into a collage of frosted wonderlands. Sometimes it was the wind, moaning and spooky, and sometimes it was angry hands that tugged at loose shutters. Or maybe it was a tormented tenant from the old days when the place was a rooming-house who paced back and forth in the attic, until the wind died and he ceased to exist, after his trip to the barn where legend had it that he had hanged himself. (Mark had kept that little bit of folklore a secret from Pam.)

It reminded Mark of the house where he grew up. He had lived in a building that had plastic storm windows and no foundation, and which was banked at ground level with sawdust and fir boughs. The wind lifted the carpet in the parlour to make a flowered piecrust, tacked down at the perimeter with galvanized shingle nails. He could remember the school mornings of standing by the kitchen stove, his back being cold even as his face burned.

"This has to be the coldest goddamn house in Canada," Pam said one morning as she drank tea while standing over a heat register which made her nightgown balloon. "I wish I had stayed in Ontario."

"Yes, it's cold, but I've seen colder," Mark said. "The house I grew up in up in Falconer was so cold that when I went to bed at night I had to put on a sailor's overcoat to keep me from freezing into a corpse. When I woke up in the mornings I could see my breath, clouds of vapour right there in the room. I puffed it out like I was smoking a cigar. That big bedroom, with its three single cots, was a steaming dung pile."

"I could never survive in a place like that. And having left it for a better life I would not have come back. I wish you had told me these things before we moved here. I would like to live in a comfortable bungalow with a picture window facing the street."

"Pam. Moving here was your idea, not mine!"

"Bullshit! You brought me here in the middle of the summer when everything was in blossom. Why didn't you tell me the winters got so dangerously cold?"

"The house will be warm when the renovations are completed. But we have to do things slowly. If we try to modernize this old place, we'd take all the character out of it. All we would have left would be a mongrel, like some I see along the road. We have to keep it authentic."

"This village is full of authentic old houses. Most are falling down and some are burning in the night."

"Pam, honey, I want to make a statement here. I want to go in my own direction. It's never out of fashion to follow one's dream. And I am not in the dark zone either!"

"Oh yes, that dream. I think it came along before you were mature, back when you were looking to impress some local people who have long since grown away from it and moved on. And who is in your secret little country circle anyway? Well, I'm not quite sure."

"I have no circle. I just appreciate the freedom of the country, a place to express my feelings and not follow the colour of the month."

"I can see there's no use arguing with you. Would you bring home some job application forms for me tomorrow? I'm going to look for work, if such a thing can be found in this neck of the woods. Mrs. Bell said she would look after Nathaniel."

"Yes, I will. I'll go to the mill office, get the forms for you. It would be good for you to get out, plus we can always use the extra money."

Pam had set out to block the parlour fireplace with a sheet of Styrofoam. As she worked she rambled on: "A spooky old mill with a leaning chimney, ghostly barns with their backs broken, houses with busted-out windows burning in the night, dilapidated churches, an Andy Griffith garage, a falling-down railway station, a boarded-up general store – everything in this village is in a state of decay and here you are trying to bring it back to the way it was a hundred years ago. And music lessons, recitals, literature – these things don't happen in the modern home. The current-day kids are into computers, hockey, tennis, and snowmobiles, not fox and geese, not spelling bees and poetry. Nathaniel has no interest in these things, he told me so. Oh, you drive me crazy sometimes!" She kicked at the Styrofoam and her eyes sparkled. "Next you'll have me dressing in a hoop-skirt, sitting in front of the fire, knitting." She pointed a finger. "I'm warning you!"

"I'll bring home some job applications tomorrow, I promise. And in the spring we'll look for a house in town, or head back to Ontario." Mark was shocked by Pam's outburst. He had never seen her release so much built-up anger; it had to be built-up because of the way it flowed out so freely. And it saddened him to think that she was suddenly against everything he dreamed of doing and that she had been keeping such feelings under cover. And he knew too that it had never really been her idea to move here; she had gone along with his wishes, the boyhood dream.

He went outside, and looked across the snowfields that were shining under a layer of crust. The buildings and fences stood frozen in the December night. He thought, Oh, how she has changed from the soft-spoken young woman from Dain City. Or has this country changed me so I don't see its realness anymore? I must sit down and have a talk with Pam. In Ontario we used to talk things out. We both have to be happy if this is going to work. Maybe after she finds a job she'll be more contented. He went back inside and approached her from behind to give her a hug. But she blocked his advance with sharp elbows.

She said, without turning around, "Would the Connors family have anything to do with our moving here to Blueberry Ridge?"

The question shocked Mark and for a moment he could not believe what he was hearing. "The Connors family? What about them?"

"They live just up the road. You went out with Sally, Mrs. Bell told me."

"Yes, we went out when she was in high school and I worked in the woods with Papa-Jo. She moved away before I went to Ontario. I believe she's in Vancouver. It's like someone you may have dated in Dain City. I don't care about them personally."

"This old village is full of surprises. But this one so near is quite a coincidence."

"So that's what's eating you."

"No, no, it's not her, not her. Mrs. Bell told me that she had dumped you good."

This statement stabbed Mark in the heart. And he had to work hard to not show his hurt.

"She said that Sally would never take you back; that you had an upriver stink on you."

"As I remember, she was a village snob," Mark said, and he thought, I know we had no bathroom in those days but we kept ourselves clean.

"And what about that ghost in the barn you never told me about? Mrs. Bell said a man had hanged himself from a beam?"

"There's no truth in that. It's just old folklore. In fact, I think the tale adds a bit of romance to the place."

"You'll never catch me anywhere near that goddamn barn again!"

Pam was right, it was a cold house, and in more ways than one. But he thought, If I can keep her contented here until the renovations are made, I think she will grow to like the place in spite of its ghosts. It is a fine balance between her faith in me and the superstitions.

On a day in January, Pam called the mill to tell Mark the oil furnace had shut off. "We need a repairman and we need him fast!" she cried.

"Honey, I'll get right on it!"

He hurried to Atlantic Rentals, borrowed a kerosene heater, and purchased a can of fuel. On his way to the farmhouse he drove too fast on a road that was smoking in snow. The pavement, under a layer of green ice, had a scum over it like the bottom of an unwashed milk bottle. And twice he almost lost control when the car skidded, end for end. When he got home he found Pam and Nathaniel sitting on the floor of the dining room with blankets wrapped around them.

"Oh, thank God," she said. "It's so cold here, so depressing. I keep waiting for something else to break, or a door to blow off its hinges."

Mark fired up the heater and set it on the floor in the centre of the kitchen near where the water pipes were. He closed the doors that led out of this room so as to keep that part of the house warm until the repairman got there. The fumes made their heads ache as they cooked supper on its little flame. It was a tedious winter night in a drafty house where an upstairs door squeaked like a coffin lid.

"When the house is fixed up, we'll look back on this as an adventure."

"Adventure," Pam snarled. "Don't talk to me about adventure!"

"In the spring, we'll head back to Ontario," he promised. "We'll get a little apartment in Virgil, jobs at McKinnon Industries."

Still, the next day, praying that he could restore her belief in the place, Mark ordered a dozen storm windows from the Eaton's mail-order catalogue. When they arrived a week later, he and a friend, using icy ladders, lifted them carefully to be screwed into place on the upstairs dormers. Some of these aluminium windows were too short and a piece of two-by-six had to be fitted upon the sill to make them reach. But it made the stairs warmer, especially if there was a wind. Nonetheless he knew it was a patch job, one that paint or any kind of plastic cement would not cover. He knew the windows would have to be replaced by thermal panes, with authentic wood frames down the road. Such was the commitment to his life's old dream.

He did these things even knowing that Pam had already packed some of her things and that she said that she would be leaving come spring, with or without him. And then he thought, Maybe she is just pretending to make a point. Because deep down, I can feel that she is growing to like the old place. Maybe it is me she wants to get rid of, which is the worst case scenario for a romantic. It was my dream after all. These thoughts, which were growing inside him like a virus, were now upsetting his days of meditation. And his poetry was suffering because of it.

He walked the chip-seal highway in the dark of night, pondering what to do. He knew he had to forget the old dream now and get to the core of the matter. Because anyone could empathize that when a woman stops sleeping with you; when she locks her bedroom door at night; when she stops eating with you, instead organizing the mealtimes for her and her son before you get home from work; when she does her and her son's laundry and leaves yours piled on the floor to be done by you at some ungodly hour; when she quits speaking to you and refuses to talk under any conditions, even when your folks come downriver to visit, you have to concede that the marriage is over and it is time to move on.

APPLE PICKING

WE HAD SEEN THEM FROM THE ROAD, WATCHED AS THE delicate pink blossoms scattered to leave pistils that soon became marbles, then plum-size apples stained green, then red, and finally a deep purple, as they hung from overweighted limbs. The old tree was in the centre of a clearing, shading a crumbling rock cellar where lilac and chokecherry trees made a hedge that had turned scarlet from the autumn frost.

We picked our way through grass that long awaited the scythe, stepped around rusted tin cans, blueberry-studded bear scat, and squeezed through the prickly, waist-high purple raspberry bush to where we stood beside the old scarred trunk. And we visualized bears smacking the tangy flavour we so desired. A woodchuck whistled to scare us off.

We found bunions on which to place our feet, climbed, fell back, and stood on shoulders, unbalanced as we reached upward for the heavily laden, kinked limbs. We were brushed by powder leaves, stabbed in the back by bear-broken branches, but reached new highs. The limbs were huge and strong – elephant trunks, knees, and thighs that supported us as we crawled, smelling tar, clinging to the gray torso that was like an old earth mother, forsaken in the outback.

You were wearing an old plaid shirt, too long in the sleeves, your tan-freckled smile radiant among the foliage, having spent the long summer days in fields of berry and bloom. Too young for love, we were partners in this outdoor game, the gathering of wild apples. This was long before I knew you as a wife, the mother of our daughter.

We had gone there after school, squeezed through a rustic iron gate, stole along to where – as in my mother's paintings – the apples were crowded like so many swollen hawthorns on their stems. And just then, too, the sun broke through between the clouds, and made a beam, as if to draw water or even goodness from the tree in which we stood, like the rays that shine on Jesus in Mass cards. Or to cast a light on us, and the forbidden fruit, like the energy that gleams through our church's stained-glass windows, backlit from the river's radiance.

It was so easy, stealing the foods of temptation, leaving our teeth marks in their skin, munching with cramped jaws the first crab apples of the season. We looked at their inner parts: stem-end to blossomed-end, their veins of red, specks of russet, varnished cavities that protected the seeds, "Queen's Choice," my mother called them.

We bounced ourselves to shake the limbs, to drop the bigger, sunburned apples to the earth, to be looked for, on forked-stems of three, in the after grass. Gathering them, some of which had been bruised by a rock or twig, we made hammocks in our shirts, so that we looked like peasant art, or a ruinous Bible scene. We spilled them in the wildflowers as we went, to be gathered again and delivered to our homes, where we unloaded them on the plank tables of our savoury-scented autumn kitchens.

"Oh my goodness, children, where did you get them?"

"At the old Vickers place of course," and I told myself not to say where if asked again. "The old Mursereau tree," I might have said, though it was resting that year. It had not been the setting that mattered, or even the apple, but the company, the love of our still-unfamiliar selves being tested for devilry in an outlying wilderness. From then on it would always be a time and place in the mind, a moment held together in a secret bond, brought forth by the taste of a crab apple.

Later we had seen the fruits of our labour hanging to dry on strings across some shed, or between the flaky crusts of pie, or perhaps honey coloured in a jar with their stems still intact. My mother had stewed them, with a touch of cinnamon and butter, for the dining room dessert. But they would never look or taste as good again as the first bite sampled, and in that company.

The taste of a crab apple takes me to you, even now.

I could say it was in the same year, the way that time compresses a thing, and the aging process distorts the past, but in counting the empty chairs and viewing the photographs on the mantel, I can see that it is three generations hence. On a Sunday in December, after the long rains of autumn, and the frost had made leaded, stained-glass panes over shallow ponds, and outside the window snowflakes are falling among the blue limbs of the oak, in a parlour in the city, I am dressed in my Sunday clothes, listening to my granddaughter stumble for the piano keys. She is to be applauded, not for her music exactly, but for who she is and what she means to me. At eight years old she is freckled, her face beaming in that way yours used to be.

The music ends, and we break for tea: a scallop-like applesauce, and homemade ice-cream served on ornate dishes to be nursed on linen napkins, eaten with silver spoons. And in this setting, as in all settings now, I think of myself as out of place. I eat, and think of you, resting in a churchyard in Black's Harbour. I see you there, so long ago, your presence holy in the music, your freckled face beaming in the branches of a tree.

APARTMENT

IN HIS SMALL APARTMENT MARK WRUNG HIS HANDS AND walked from window to window. On the front side was the bay with its little sailboats and the sounds of bigger vessels, their decks piled with lobster traps, as they chugged out to sea. To the back was a city street with its hum of traffic. He had his books on a shelf, a few 1960s movie posters, and a three-legged couch that a furniture company had given him because of its defect. He had bought a chrome table and two chairs at the Salvation Army's Thrift Shop. In the spare bedroom he made up a cot in the event that his son came to stay. But he doubted if this would happen as his little place was shabby, its whereabouts, as compared to Blueberry Ridge, boring with no woods, streams, or fields in which to ramble. To keep his sanity, he walked night and morning. This was a power-walk that started his blood pumping and helped clear his mind. I took the high road, he thought. It was the only thing I could do and keep my sanity. Still, to look back caused him great sadness because he knew he had failed as a husband and father, although he figured the low road would have put him under the ground. How did I let my relationship with Pam get so toxic? he mused.

And then he thought, You know what, I am a statistic. I'm part of a bigger movement where the traditional family – a man and woman married with children living under one roof – has become a thing of the past. The modern-day family is more loosely connected. They give each other freedom to do things that make them whole and are not bound to a spouse's wants and needs. They communicate through smart-phones. In that sense, Pam is kilometres ahead of me in her way of thinking, just as Mrs. Anderson, single for fifty years, had been decades ago. For a moment he thought he was part of a revolution, a turning point in history, and he felt a touch of pride. There would be a poem, maybe even an essay in this. It had been a crazy summer where the old ways went off the rails and everyone's ideas, be they selfish, abrasive, or even emotionally cruel, became the norm. And when it was over, all concerned needed some form of counselling to help them get on the new track.

He thought, There was a time, even in my own day, where the family, old and young, lived and worshipped together. We worked the land and were happy in our collective notions of what we stood for. When the old people got worn out, the children stepped up and took their places in the fields and woods. We worked in harmony and were all a part of a bigger rural soul. We loved one another in our rugged ways, because our livelihood and the natural things that our lives depended upon – the animals, trees, river, and earth – demanded it. "Earth is the right place for love," Robert Frost had said in a poem. The sharing of these things made our communities kinfolk. Now it is time for the old mentality to break apart. I have watched it happen. First there came the depreciation of the farm, because it was impossible to live off the land in the modern day, hippy fads be damned. The fields were let go fallow. Then our trees were gobbled up by corporations from foreign lands and shipped offshore for processing. (These people never plant a tree.) The river's value as a transporter of material and a food source became a place for rich vacationers to play with what was left of our salmon stocks. Our belief in the divinities and the old traditions also faded, leading to the demise of the country church and one-room school. And there was the scattering of families, the breaking up of community circles. It is all a kind of revolution.

For the modern woman, freedom now fills her mind with a new-found sense of wonder. She has finally broken clear of the old communal ways, the slavery of cooking and cleaning for a dozen men. These people want to be independent and have learned to fly solo. I applaud them for their courage and smarts. But I am an old-fashioned traditionalist and no longer sure I can find my right mind anymore. Because when you are raised in the country in a big family circle, it comes as second nature to follow their ways and beliefs. Oh, how I would like to go back to the old Falconer life, not to spend my time thinking of school and church traditions, for nostalgia has a dangerous brushstroke of its own, not to drink and party my life away, but just to live in that happy place. Back then I was gleeful because we were young and all experiences were original and earth-shattering. Why does one work and study so hard to escape from the person they really are? Why does one isolate one-self from that love and togetherness? Do all romances end with marriage? Do all marriages end with achievement? Do all modern marriages end in divorce? They appear to be so short-lived any-more. Why do we always grasp for a happiness that does not exist? Or is chasing after a dream where the romance lies?

Although everyone said that old Joseph Moore – no one upriver had an ounce of use for him – was hard on his boys and showed no mercy for anyone who could not carry his weight physically or mentally without being called a half-wit, he *was* family. Mark recalled a time when his father asked him to walk in the rain with the horse from Picket Brook to Falconer, over twenty-five miles, and how he said, "Yes, Papa" and how because of his allergies he had coughed and sneezed all the way. He remembered arriving home well into the night short of breath, and the old man say-ing, "What the Christ kept you so long? Ya lame-arse jeezer" and he gave Mark a swift kick in the seat of his pants. You had to be strong to endure a parent like that. Mark wondered how much of his father was in him and if he had been hard on his own family.

He thought of the time he scolded his son Nathaniel for missing a partridge because he had not aimed the shotgun. He had called his son "stupid." And Nathaniel had cried because he felt he had let his father down. It was a delicate moment, where for a split

second, Mark saw Papa-Jo in himself. So he embraced Nathaniel
and said he was sorry, and that he had missed birds too at times
when the food was more needed. But he could see a hurt in his
son's eyes. It was a pain that came right through the generations.

Now, this memory troubled Mark and he wished
he could have the moment back. He remembered shed-
ding tears in the church on the day of his son's high school
graduation. It was the first breakthrough, finally, by a Moore
into a different society, maybe even university – a feather in
all their hats. And he remembered weeping in church on the
day of his mother's funeral. She had been the selfless one who
inspired him to push forward in spite of the odds. He remembered the priest saying that when the doctor went into
Dorothy Moore's hospital room, held her hand, and told her she
had less than a week to live, she hugged him and apologized.
"I'm sorry I had to put you through this, dear," she said. "It would
not have been an easy morning for you either."

This was another reason why Mark categorized Mama-Jo as
a saint.

Now, as he rambled in the hope-filled sunshine, he tried to
relate to the cityscape, find his soul as he had been able to do in
the country. He looked at buildings, most of which were shabby
and unfriendly, their doors and windows barred. And he wondered
if there would be a mood day when he would be able to con-
nect to this scenery like he was able to do in the country. Would
the bleakness of the town inspire a Dickens moment, perhaps at
Christmastime with snowflakes coming down, where the shabby
buildings and poverty of spirit could be drawn upon? Would it be
a Shakespeare incident where some long-awaited tragedy unfold-
ed, the outer tempest identifying the more turbulent inner storm?
He thought of *King Lear*. "Who's there, besides foul weather?" For
a moment Mark looked at commercial buildings, some of which
had little balconies, as troubled places. He could hear wrangling inside, people dickering over a few pennies. And he wondered if he
would be able to find his own spirit in a setting that was built for

commerce, for he had been a landscape lover and a patron of the arts and that was where his soul remained. He would have to drive to the country, get out and walk, recapture his inspiration. He loved the woods in autumn, especially the gold-leafed birches and the white pines that shed their needles in showers of orange.

Sometimes for a break, he drove to Falconer where he and his brother Toots went for a walk in the forest. They stopped by a brook in that old deer-hunting, pulpwood-cutting country-side, boiled water for tea, and ate sandwiches, while admiring the moose-birds – with their small sad voices – that ate from their hands. And they smoked cigarettes in the way they had done years before when working with Papa-Jo. Mark found there was great healing power in the water and trees, as well as the music of birds that carried in their melodies so much of his youth, an innocent time before Pam came into his life. After one of those outings, a good feeling stayed with him for a few days. When it was gone from his mind and he became troubled once more, he phoned his brother to do it again because he was the only family he trusted enough to unload his miseries upon, until, sensing his brother was bored, he stopped calling, because Toots had no similar experiences to relate, no troubles from which to heal, not here at home where he had spent his whole life, alone, uneventful, and all his days, with dreams beyond reach, had long been discarded. His brother still lived in that day, rather than try to escape it, and so had no illusions, glorified by memory, in which to return. Because you have to leave a thing before you can look back upon it with any kind of romance, or its godparent, nostalgia.

"Let it all go," the counsellors had told him. "Never risk your own well-being for the sake of a property. That old house might have looked like a castle to you, but to everyone else it was just another place on the side of the road, and it is a long way from town. Eventually there will be no one living in these outlands. All the trends are towards city life. Plus, your sanity has to come first. And do not let your mental fatigue incline you toward materialism. You, a poet, should understand – better than most – that there are no internal rewards in going down the mainstream road. There is no heritage in old buildings that could burn or fall down tomorrow. A legacy comes out of the mind, not the place. And it is better for the boy if you go and leave him in the home with his mother. Legally you are entitled to sell the house and take half the money. But you have to be able to sleep at night too." Mark remembered that conversation as if it had been this very day. And he knew he would never forget the day he had left the old tree-shaded farmhouse.

He thought of his last walk around what had become her house, the grass having been clipped, the flowers watered just one day before. He opened the barn doors and looked in. A bit of history: a long-shafted wheelbarrow, the spinning wheel ... For a moment his boyhood came back and he was sorry he had to leave the dream, let go of what he thought was important at that time in his life. Dreams of all ages should be fulfilled, he thought.

He admired the bay window with the flat piano inside. It was like the picture he had seen in a school book where Beethoven played the *Moonlight Sonata* on a stormy winter night, or the Mozart family, with little seven-year-old Wolfgang playing the spinet while his sister Maria Anna sang. Though the culture of old traditions was not really his own, he had been working to establish it, hoping to attract the scholars he felt would gravitate around him, trying to develop the social pretensions that would help him compete with those who thought they were better because they came from away, full of the artless vanity of their conceit. Or the ones who had left because they felt the place and the people were not good enough for them, and whom he knew would always praise their own inarticulateness as a virtue.

He looked at the end of the house where the library was supposed to be added on, a part of the bigger plan, the walls of books – his next project. (Yes, that would have set tongues wagging in Blueberry Ridge.) He envisioned it as an authentic add-on, with its spool-railing balcony, the wood deck-chairs, the awnings, the French windows with their green shutters laid open, and with the family inside where they gathered around the piano while Nathaniel played *Für Elise* for his grandparents. In the upstairs hallway hung *Lilacs in a Vase*, a work he had commissioned the artist Richard Howe to paint. These were the things that Pam had described as "trying to be high-toned and yuppy."

He could remember hugging the corner of the house, now already a part of her. He hugged the old oak tree. He hugged Nathaniel, already a bigger part of Pam's world, and could feel his heart beating, like when you hold a wounded bird in your hand. Or maybe it was a reliving of those asthma attacks from the old days, less painful but more lonesome. He remembered getting into the truck, starting the engine. He sat there for a long time, the engine rattling as if to hurry him along. He could not think. He turned off the ignition, got out, and hugged his son again, while taking one last look at the place. There was a shutter on the upstairs window above the veranda that needed paint. "Nathaniel, tell your mother."

"Yes, Daddy, I'll tell her!"

He stood beside his son, so close he could feel the warmth from his soul, sense the anguish that oozed from his pores; pain that mixed with his own, to become one big hurt they shared but which arose now suddenly from opposite standpoints. Both pains were reflected in each other's eyes, mysterious and already inaccessible. He had to be strong, put up a shield, block out his son's love for him. Block out his love for the son. He got back into the truck, started the engine, and drove slowly out the lane and on down the highway, leaving Nathaniel standing on the lawn, looking forlorn and empty while the old home place grew smaller and smaller until it disappeared in the rear view mirror, and only its clay chimney pots were visible above the trees. This experience would haunt him for the rest of his life. And he dreamed of big old houses and Nathaniel every night.

Sometimes now, though it was not easy, he drove to Blueberry Ridge, slowed down to pass his former farmhouse, and on back to the lane where a damp chill spread across the reedy pasture, baked hard by the autumn sun and winds, and a thick layer of preserver's wax covered the drinking trough. Snow-clouds drifted low and a wind tossed lupine sentinels that were stiff as haywire. There was an organ-like moaning in the power lines. He walked on a path worn smooth by cows and turned toward the treed line fence. He tried to grasp the old moorland poetic spirit, recapture the earth feelings he enjoyed before his world crumbled. (He could recall his wife on the day of their wedding. In her long white dress, she had been riding a bicycle through fields of daisies, the long train billowing in the breeze. That image had stayed with him longest.) Now in the distance he could see the house's chimneys where smoke arose and hung in a cloud that resembled a cocoon. He tried to put a finger on where things went off the rails.

In cold weather in town, he might have desired a certain woman, a classic debutante to warm his soul, instil him with confidence. But he knew she would come without a heartfelt intimacy, because of her town-bred lack of melancholy, her indifference to nature, which any woman would have to be conscious of to be at one with his heart, even if she offered him more intellectual freedom to observe a landscape that controlled his moods and his muse, show a little desire as opposed to apathy, embrace a pine tree, identify a bird's spirit. On winter nights, some isolated town apartment would be fine if the woman in question had the right sensitivity and was with him emotionally, at least until her perception of him had changed.

Once he went to the door of a woman who had tried to seduce him years before. He knocked and called out the name "Karen." But an old man answered, saying that woman was long gone from the place.

When Mark was not walking briskly about town, he played classical music on his CD player. These were concertos, sonatas, and quartets that Pam had not appreciated so he had kept them in the glove compartment of his car. Now he played them whenever the mood came along. He sat by a window and looked out at the sparkling bay with its waves tossing the little boats at the marina and listened to Beethoven, Bach, and Wagner and he drifted with the melodies. There was something comforting in the combination of wind, water, and music that set his mind at peace – until with a tingle, it drifted back to Blueberry Ridge where the dining room table was laid for a family feast. And it was hard for Mark not to feel sorry for himself.

In the evenings, he heard car horns and the squealing of tires from the street in back of his apartment. And the cups and saucers in his cupboard jingled when the big Ocean trains laboured past, their dull whistles echoing off the bay with the hollowness of a funeral knell. There was a pub not far from his fire escape, from where bad music could be heard pulsating off his window glass. Twisted shadows danced in the smoky light and reflected upon his bedroom wall. It is sad what has become of music, he thought. Sometimes out of desperation he went there for a nightcap and met women whom he felt he could have dated. And from this spiritual lift, for a brief moment, he thought of himself as The Great Gatsby. But after a drink and a few babbling words, he found these people to be of no interest to him. Besides, still living in the miseries of his failed marriage he felt vulnerable and in no mental condition to look for a woman. It would take a long while to heal, if ever. Sometimes he went to the pub for breakfast because from his window he could smell bacon frying. There, he sat in a back corner, drank coffee, and read the morning newspapers. The waitresses were very kind to him, and for a time he thought of himself as Ernest Hemingway in Paris in the 1920s.

Using these literary connotations he was able to tolerate the apartment. But he knew he would have to buy himself a mini-home, a property that would give him some return on his money. These things would be sorted out in the weeks ahead. At least he still had a job at the mill.

THE RETURN

UPON MY RETURN FROM THE WEST, HAVING SPENT twenty-one years, five weeks, and three days working in the oil fields, I drive around Bradford and head upriver, past the torn-down pulp mill, the empty lumber yards, and on up the original roadstead, now quite abandoned due to an extended bypass. This is the highway that I drove to and from work on during those years when I worked at the mill and lived in the Robertson house in Blueberry Ridge. The road is in need of repair, with potholes and long patches of rough asphalt. Beyond the ditches, the houses, some of which I used to think were fine places, are crowded with shrubbery, their sheds that ring around dooryards, sunken. The small fields are standing waist-high in goldenrod, their gray blossoms ragged on the stems, like cotton candy or witch's broom. It is a great letdown from the canvas I had primed from memory: autumn in the air, the old-world fragrance of plowed land, men and boys stooping to gather the unearthed potatoes. ,

There is an all-terrain vehicle racing along on what had once been the railway bed. I smell the warm gravel and for a moment I am twelve years old and collecting marble-size stones so that if I see a partridge or a squirrel, both of which are fair game, I can go after it with my slingshot. The scent of railway gravel (heated by the sun) belongs to the old home place, as does the fragrance of burning leaves, which brings back the landscape from stories and poems of the new grade readers: "The Great Stone Face," "The Legend of Sleepy Hollow," "The Highwayman" – metaphors from a day when I could smell bonfires from my bedroom windows, hear the echo of hunters' deer rifles as I did my homework, or should have done my homework. That old picture gallery is still in these scents and sounds. For a moment I want to go back and live in that sweet old mindset, before my misguided life's ambitions entered into it.

As I drive, there are noisy blue jays that flit about the hawthorn trees, that school-days bird whose screams could be heard inside the classroom even with the door closed. *And all the day the blue jay calls throughout the autumn land.* They had been Wilfred Campbell moments. I still think of the blue jay as a voice more than a bird, the voice of youth, the voice of freedom, the voice of a waning summertime.

Of course in those days, I viewed the world solely from our farmstead, the outside world being a haze of uncertainty. At that time and place, greatness meant not necessarily progressing, but just keeping out of trouble, hiding that part of ourselves that could lead us to embarrassment, even recriminations. "The Moore family have become respectable," I once overheard a woman from the village say in the post office. "We seldom hear their names mentioned anymore."

Save for the symbols that appear out of a scent or a sound, the years have diminished the visibility that emerges from this country road. Perhaps it is part of the healing process, for it is said that we miss only what we can remember, and after so many years away the "unseen" remains buried. Maybe it is all for the better.

Now, the drive from town to my tree-shaded farmhouse seems shorter, because of the road's emptiness, the lack of imaginative powers to inflate the images. I try to grasp that driving-home-from-the-mill state of mind, from when things were good, like a moment brought forth from an old song on the radio. But I find this part is beyond anything I can reimagine. Because there are no symbols left from the early adult years, no spirits that will free themselves; nothing that has not been imprisoned, let go, and locked up again; no release of emotions from a time so traumatic it had to be buried with a spade, smoothed over with

a garden rake and tramped upon with a sledgehammer for as-
suredness. And a whole lot of counselling and meditation. The
community is like an abandoned pasture. Nothing offers up the
old appetite. And I suppose that is for the better. And I know that
Falconer, fifteen miles up the river, will be even harder for me to
reach.

The fact that I am driving toward the place in Blueberry
Ridge, in the sunset, the landscape changing with the hues of the
evening, adds to the despair of the countryside. So many little
houses – of hard-working people I had known – have fallen to decay, their windows busted out, dooryards having grown over with
shrubbery. And the ancient trees are bunioned and gnarled from
years of abuse. They stand at the edge of the road like elderly people, hunched and twisted and in need of walking canes. No doubt
some have been broken down or forever stained by the wrath of
winter storms.

All the bigger farmhouses – the Anderson mansion, the Connors place, the Bell property – have disappeared. Only their rock
foundations are visible in the tall untrammelled grass. The schoolhouse that my son attended for eight years has been boarded up
with weather-beaten sheets of plywood and there is a jungle of
shrubbery growing in the playground. In fact, vegetation has overtaken the fences and is crowding into the main road. The service
station is gone as is the post office and the general store. The little
three-windowed, clapboard church, St. Andrew's Anglican, with its
windows now backlit from the sun, is no longer in use, the priest
having moved on, I am told, to a professorship after disgracing the
church with an extra-marital relationship and a remarriage of his
own. Good for him.

When my brothers and I were small, and again with my
ex-wife and son, we went to that humble little church on Sunday
mornings, with its pump organ, three-woman choir, and handful
of poorly dressed parishioners. And I used to wish that I were in a
city cathedral with a pipe organ and a Bach choir, a place where I
could rub shoulders with influential people. At that time, I felt that

a place without some elitism and a few successful artisans would be a community not worth living in. But years later in "the West," when I got to attend the city basilica, among high-brow strangers, listening to the best of spiritual music from the most polished of instruments, I would have given all I owned for a moment back in the pew with my young family. It is funny how life and the aging process have switched my priorities. The things I thought were unimportant when I was a young man are entities that I grieve for now that I am old. And what I thought to be the right priorities back then have now became meaningless. I think that Pam (my ex-wife) had been right to move on shortly after she first saw the dark side of me. I should have listened to her and not have been obsessed with a dream that had been spun out of poverty, a delusion that took me into a time zone of the previous century.

But when it comes to the devastation of the "external" landscape – for I am a nature lover first and last – and the decay of symbols from a once vibrant farm community, I wonder if it is fair to blame it on a government that has been in power for such a short few years? Had the scent of oil in the West and the lure of a few quick dollars destroyed this end of what had once been a great farming nation?

Here and there I stop and talk with someone, perhaps an Asian who is working in his or her front yard. Possibly they have come here through the Foreign Worker Program and have stayed. But of course no one living along this highway knows who I am or cares a damn. Thank God for the aging process in that regard. No one knows that I am now unwell, with a monitor on my heartbeats and an oxygen supplement. No one knows that I have spent some years in a sanatorium after losing my job and going on a drinking binge.

So why would I try to dig up a troubled past, relive any of those past embarrassments?

It is like I have to return to see how much of the place is real or if it is mostly a dream that has now been smothered by years of medication.

I have always found that goodbyes were difficult, but now I realize that returns, after so long, are even harder to get my head around, because in my mind, leaving here was supposed to have been forever. The countryside around the highway is much more ragged than the one in my memory, especially those last days when I hated to leave, because I thought it was a paradise. It is like the past is a foreign country that one should not revisit, literally. But I suppose, like my own circumstance, there is no one to blame for this once beautiful farm country having fallen into a state of dereliction. (Pam had seen this coming long before I did.) The by-pass perhaps, the mill closures, the god-damned government – it is never the local people. The rural soul is never wrong about any-thing, according to Homer. Although to meet those loving family members again, vibrant and young as they once were, even in this shabby setting, would challenge any philosopher's theory. For what is a landscape without its mood-setting people, but a wasteland, trees, wildflowers, and beautiful sunsets be dammed?

Everything has vanished, except the house I so affection-ately called Wayside. I had not realized how small that house was, even with the added bay window and verandas. And even now, so many years later, I can picture it with the add-on library and fam-ily room, a piping wood stove in the rear, and a couch by the wood box, things I had planned to construct as part of the overall. resto-ration. But now, with the barn gone, the old house stands without pretensions among ancient trees, the forlorn upstairs dormers look-ing out through foliage, like four-panelled mirrors, framed by kinked limbs, the gables rising above a hamlet of leaves. The windows ap-pear blinded against the outside world, where a woodpecker chops on a poplar skeleton, the adjacent rolling pastures a forest of ever-greens. The hedge that I had once kept trimmed has gone wild, as has the veranda and chimney ivy. It is hard to see the old place from the highway, even though someone has put a shiny tin roof over top the cedar shingles, the latter twisted and bent at the eaves.

It is like looking at a woman I had once perceived to have been beautiful, but who has let herself not so graciously shrink into old age. Or when you look at your own reflection in a car window and suddenly you are shorter and fatter and with legs that are bowed out of all proportion. Perhaps it was my imagination that made the house what it was, a resourcefulness without which any kind of romance, even nostalgia, could have survived. And with an even more uncertain destiny which serves to provoke an august reflection of indifference. And I am glad that my legacy is not hanging on this derelict, but on my poetry publications, however humble.

I cannot help but wonder what state of mind I would have been in had I stayed on the narrower path, kept my head to the grindstone. How would I have dealt with the emotions made stronger from repression? How would I have achieved my dream without that ingenuity, having reduced my priorities to this crumbling state of materialism? Or worse, having moved to live in a shoebox in town. There is a certain handicap that comes with having grown up on a farm, a place destined to fail because of the changing times, and having tried to reinvent and live in the past. It is a dangerous pastime. And – as I found out – there is a greater demoralization still in trying to make love happen with a woman against her wishes, a person who did not really know who I was, as I did not know myself, at the time of our marriage.

I park at some distance on the now shadowy chip-seal road and, using my cane, walk past the house. I try to grasp the dream I nurtured before things turned sour with Pam, what I would do in poetry, even the secret prospect of inn-keeping. I have to concentrate, really concentrate – because the mind has a way of deleting troubled times: betrayal with breakfast, resentment with lunch, anger with dinner, jealousy with dessert, of talking to oneself on those outdoor walks while clutching for a life – before I can even comprehend that this was the world of a stranger whose name was Mark Moore. I say stranger, because I and the one in those memories have long since stopped being the same person. We have the same names, nothing more. I guess you could say that I am his upshoot, sprung from the life he fertilized in his own humble way, during the immaturity of youth. The Mark Moore of that time made no mistakes; everything was perfection because he was on his way to quintessence. And I think too that arrogance can always find its virtue along that crooked road of reflection.

Suddenly, I realize that the landscape from down home can never live up to the images left by its absence. Time and distance have distorted a picture that, through familiarity, may have kept its grandeur. Still, as I walk, I can feel the presence of my brothers Toots and Sacker, now long dead, and Nathaniel, who has changed his name and sex, and is somewhere on the road. I can also remember the old dog I buried in the grove, how he ran in circles as we went, Nathaniel and I, for an evening of trout fishing in that lonely stream. But there is no trace of the young woman I married in Niagara. The years of counselling have eliminated her and our disagreements and the scars from trying to cling to them. And I think that is why there is no classicist view left in this picture. You have to have a dream world and dream people to live in it. Otherwise the whole cognition is overtaken with realness, the not-so-spirited gray world of routine, the calamities and death of real life. For me, fact is not the sweetest dream that labour knows.

Further along, I leave the road and cut through what had once been fields. Not even ghosts of the cattle remain, the trees having turned it from pasture to wood, and with a woods spirit. Along the fence there are mountain ash, hawthorn berries red as fire, and apples hanging like bait on bowed fishing poles, the slanting sunlight casting a Biblical light on the scene. I stretch a thin arm and the blue veins in my wrist tighten like fiddle strings, the bough bending as I jerk an apple from its delicate hold. I don't think I'm abusing the tree. It seems more a case of the tree abusing me. I sample the apple, recalling the taste from years ago and the images that came out of their flavour when they were baked after the evening meal. (This is the best connection to my old place so far.) And suddenly the young family is beside me, eager to share the fruit, partake in another of life's new experiences. I find that because I am inclined to melancholy, this part is hard to recollect without sentiment. And I wonder if I am not opening wounds that took years to heal over. And then I think, with my last prognosis, what do I have to lose? I will not be around in two or three years anyway.

I make my way into the bigger woods. So tall are the trees it appears I am going to be enshrouded in darkness. I am looking for a rock that marked the place where I buried the dog. It is all so different, the trees so much bigger. Then I come upon a cross, made of decaying boards as high as my head. It is swaying in a hollow wind as though it were being dangled by some invisible puppeteer, and on the verge of collapsing. And then the rock which is covered with red maple leaves. On the cross are the dates, barely legible, remembering the dog's passing and these dates also coincide with my leaving.

I feel the cross had been erected by Nathaniel, as a memorial to the dog, yes, but also to his father who vanished from his life that fall. The cross is too big to simply mark the place where a dog was buried. (We had settled for a rock, my son and I.) For a moment, understanding how art meditates on bereavement, I think of how life must have been for Nathaniel at that time, concluding that what I sacrificed in sentiment was a lot more than what I gained in substance, or indeed prominence. As I try to come to terms with this, the trees crowd around me. And I think of how easily it might *not* have happened – how little common sense it might have taken, on my part, to secure the family tree, that way of life and its people that have vanished before me. Because I went away on that fall evening and I didn't come back.

FIRST SNOW

I HAVE NOT HAD TIME TO WANDER IN THE AUTUMN fields and reflect on the long summer past or to pick holly or rose-hip berries and decorate the mantel. I have not had time to savour those dark days of autumn rain, to walk the sodden forest floor and leave footprints that turn black when the sun touches them. Nor have I had a chance to ride our little horse Prince on the fields of stubble, down by the river where the scent of woodsmoke hangs in the fog-heavy air. (I always do more riding in the late fall when the air is hollow and hoof beats are loud upon the frozen earth – like in the movies – the horse snorting and galloping to jump the rail fences. In my saddle it is like sitting in a rocking chair.) Nor did I witness the exodus of our Canada geese, as they flew southwest up the river, their wavering V-shaped trains, like the tails of kites, held together with invisible twine. And I ask myself, "Where have the seasons gone?"

At the beginning of winter, my father and I push to have the fall jobs completed before the snow comes. On the north side of the house, in alleys between buildings, wind breaks are erected with old storm doors and scraps of board being nailed to scantling to make the yard a kind of fortress against the approaching winds. While the hens are still free-ranging, the ground has been frozen for some time, the grass like an old man's hair, white and kinked and quite unruly, especially in the mornings when the hoar frost is heaviest. The only sounds are the chatter of the red squirrel in the tall and needleless juniper, now as black as charcoal in the dark frozen swamp, and the two-fold gulp of a raven, which Father says is the sign of foul weather, for he knows the vocabulary of this forsaken bird. Those beautiful trees had been a deep pastel in spring, pea-green in high summer, and as orange as an autumn bonfire before the spills dropped to make a scum over the smelly, black bog.

In our '55 Chevy, driving from the village on that chip-seal road that turns to gravel at the Hennessy corner, the trays of ice shine red in the sunset. Behind the car, dead leaves swirl from gutter to gutter, like the ghosts of witches. And the clouds in the downriver sky are brass, baked with flames, as in my father's paintings. But too soon this sky fades and becomes a mountain range of pink wool, above which stands a red beach ball, with a haze encircling it. The waning moon becomes transparent, like the scale of a fish, before disappearing below the hills. (We stop at the railway crossing, where a winking red light tinkles, and we watch the train with its lighted windows go past, on down the grade, toward the village. And I think what fun it would be to ride on that big train.) As Daddy drives on, I can see the dark fields – with the ghosts of men clutching the reins of horses behind their plows – and under the cow-shade pine trees, cushions of orange needles, the gray cedar rail fences now purple in the post-sunset. These are the lifeless fields of the approaching winter.

When we get home, there is a gray pall over the farm and a church organ moans in the power lines. And there is a cracking and snapping in the car's overheated radiator. The swamp having been frozen for some time, there is a further sign of precipitation, a tea-coloured overflow at the edge of the field where as a small girl I learned to skate by pushing a kitchen chair. As we unload our marketing from the car, the sky turns darker, and there is a black wind that pushes up the trail-bushed river. "There is no place like home," I say to Mother. The old farmhouse speaks to me just now, with its flowered wallpaper, the worn oilcloth floor with a coat thrown at the base of the door to keep out the draft, the night's water sitting in pails on the washstand, the wood boxes filled, the outside doors closed and buttoned down. There is a welcoming comfort here in this dell of security.

In the kitchen and living room, I build up the fires; I suppose this is a psychological reaction to storm fear. Later in the evening Mother and I play cards, while Father walks about the house, a pipe in hand, singing Jimmie Rodgers songs. He is lifting his head – like a hen drinking – as he tries to yodel. And we applaud him for his homely attempts. He had been a country singer in the old days and keeps his talent alive by performing around home. Sometimes when the light is good he stands in the living room or in his bedroom and paints the landscape he sees from the window that overlooks our home river.

When Father, Mother, and Grandmother have gone upstairs to bed, I lay on the kitchen stove couch, roll and smoke a cigarette – from Father's tobacco – while listening to the late Saturday night music out of Nashville, Tennessee, as is my habit. The song "Blueberry Hill" is a hit this fall.

I suppose I should have gotten Mrs. Kelly down the road to give me a haircut. I should have dressed up in my best jeans and boots, stayed in the village, and attempted to meet new people, then walked back home in the storm. Because it is the weekend, young people are strolling about the sidewalks, from diner to diner, their musical voices chanting to fill the evening with the youthful pleasures of a Saturday night. But I am still at the age where I crave, more than a hug or a kiss, more than a dance beside a too-loud jukebox, a beautiful sunset, a tall glass of lemonade, or a horseback ride on the frozen Mosquito Flats. My principal attribute right now is my love for the land and sky. Like most country girls, I am never bored in my own company and I am still happy in my home environment. I am at that wonderful age when childhood is coming to a close and my teen years await me. Perhaps I should be restless, but I am not.

Because of this, I know that in town I would be on the wrong side of the social activities, lost and reaching, like a lilac blossom chasing after a bumblebee, or a car running after a dog.

Indeed it's a circle I would not be welcomed into. And I would feel out of place, a solemn state that is mine when I try to mingle where I do not belong, or where I feel uncomfortable. Country people, many of whom are loners, feel this way when it comes to socializing, where town people enjoy their own circle of friends – the ones they grew up and went to school with – and who can detect the self-deprecation in a country girl, and sometimes even inquire after their troublesome relations. It is a place where a little money can spoil human behaviour, as the town people defend their own shortcomings with a hint of protectionism.

Occasionally, I arise from the sofa long enough to get myself a cup of tea from the singing kettle, put a stick of hardwood in the firebox while a north wind is making the stove pipes creak. Sparks pop from the damper to send chimney smoke low into the howling night air to create a cocoon, a conspiracy against the approaching storm. And I worry if perhaps a chimney fire is in the making.

Sometime in the night it comes, at first in tiny bits of rice and broken glass, bouncing off the doorstep and veranda floor, hopping in a kind of fairy dance – miniature doilies, stars, webs of cotton, down, fleece, cotton batting, whipped cream, and hail – blowing across our window-lighted dooryard, clinging to the old apple tree and the gables of the barn. It strikes our window glass with a *ping*, telling me to "get up, come quick, have a look – it's snowing out."

Rising from the sofa, I can see it dancing in the lights of passing cars, scudding chaff-like in the beams, boiling up the rear in clouds that drift across our fields to make little snakes that twist among the corn stubble, puffing off roofs to paint our buildings on the north side white, as it has already done to the road, and change the season from fall to winter overnight. And among them, little working carousels hurry with star-like flakes to the mournful sounds of the wind, like cranked-up toys, or things that cannot speak but play a tune, the dazzling snow puffing off roofs to create characters from fables. Some are bearded wizards, and some are Uncle Sams or Father Times, old philosophers with witches' hair frosted white like the pocket-handkerchiefs that magicians use to keep us in a spell.

Even when I press my face against the teary pane, peering through icicles that hang from the eave, our old gray barn is lost from view. I can feel the storm in the creak of garden branches, the wind's slamming of forgotten doors, the gusts that set wind chimes crazy. The snow and wind brings forth the roar of trees – like pistol shots – from having had their branches buckle under the weight, the feathery birches bending to their knees like so many horses drinking from a spring hole. Others are sighing deeply and waving like tall brushes that sweep the sky. A log shifts on the fire, and there is a rattling and chiming of the clock.

And thus goes the three-seasoned landscape, I think. In a few short minutes, all colours of the earth have been traded for white, the artistic sky having become angry, to fade into grays and blacks. And I am living in a world of snow. I get dressed in Father's old sheepskin coat and beaver cap, and set out on a long walk, across the summer pasture – with its ghosts of Prince cropping – back along an old wood road, as I have often done on winter nights, to catch the spirit, the energy of the storm and wood, the childish joys of having the wet flakes tickle my face, the wind tug at the vagabond in me, puffing up my winter clothes, like the straw people we set on verandas for Halloween. The frozen moss crunches under my feet to make porcelain boot marks. For a moment I sit on a log and watch the snow falling around me, like a stampede of cattle, bending the dead bracken under its driving hooves. At such times I like to challenge the wind and snow. "Go face them and fight them,/ Be savage again," as the Hamlin Garland poem goes. Everyone has their own idea of paradise.

Walking back to the house on tracks already covered with new flakes, I go straight to bed and dream of walking in the woods on stormy nights, of riding Prince in a foot of new snow that sprays from his hooves and from which he bends to get a taste. But it is not a deep sleep, rather a restless state of repose, with an underlying fear of the wind that howls at my window and rattles the shutters. Don't be afraid, I tell myself.

In the morning, my grandmother sits in her rocking chair and knits, her nervous face coppered by reflections of the fire. She is wearing plaid bedroom slippers, a floor-length flannel skirt, and two sweaters. Her wire-framed spectacles are luminous, her faded blue eyes fixed upon the needles clicking in her hands. With her bundled hair that glistens like silver, and her stoutness, she resembles the portraits we see of an aged Queen Victoria. She teeters in the chair, hums an old hymn, and works her tired and bony fingers as though to complete whatever it is she's making before the storm ends – as though she has a mission, even now, to grasp a new design, a new pattern, an inspiration from the spirit of the storm that has released her from habit. She is religious to the point of intolerance and can speak some Latin, she says. Although I don't believe it is Latin, or Greek either. But how would I know? I tell myself that she probably *believes* and works to hide her anxiety, block out her thoughts of real winter coming down.

But then, as though it has a mind of its own – or some divine power gets into it – the ball of yarn resting on her embroidery frame falls upon the floor from an unexpected pull and rolls across the linoleum, as if in a moment stolen from the vigilance of children to bring out the worst in her, get her out of the spell. "Oh sweet Jesus, the devil's here today," she says. In her agitation she stamps her feet and, with a grimace that reveals her false teeth, gets up and spears it with a needle. Then she settles back to carry on the hymn and what she makes. It is like she needs a purpose, a relief from her anxiety, an occupation to get her through these early winter days. She coughs, as old people do in the mornings. But the storm gives her the incentive and the energy to carry on. Don't stop working, it might have said. Stay the course, Grammy.

From the twinkle in her eyes, I think she's looking back to when she was a girl, to the handsome young companion in her life still living there. (She would not dance to just anyone's fiddle and wanted perfection in a partner, a travelling salesman from the

North Shore.) Shortly after they were married in 1896, he had gone to Ontario to start a business. But he never came home. Nor did he write a letter to state his intentions. Yet he still lives inside her, the same handsome young man. She sees the early parts of the marriage as being the best of her life. It is all so long ago, it's like a dream: those days before he went away, the memory she has glorified with time, that place to which she wishes to return when winter falls. She was so young. And I think that too much time is wasted in loneliness, that inner life which no one but she really knows. There are times now, with an air of indifference towards us all, she gets angry and cries for no reason. But I am too young to comprehend what this storm, her forsaken dream-maker, does for her and what she really means when she says, "I am old as the hills. God spare me through the long winter."

Until the knitting slips from her hands again as she has fallen into a shallow sleep. And I think that at her age, when her fanaticism stops and she has no project, she will be sitting dead.

In the upstairs hall by the heat pipe, my mother is hunched over the sewing machine, piecing together the red, black, and yellow patches of clothes that we have all worn in former times. She has a thimble and coloured threads, her glasses pushed forward on her nose as she pumps the pedal of the sewing machine, as though she is being influenced by a noise the wind is making in the pipes. This patch quilt, her handiwork, is a kaleidoscope of family scents and events, personalities that come together in a provisional picture album, a keepsake that will have been influenced by the people she loves, her melancholy views, and inspired by the uncertainty of the moment. She will stay with this as long as she can, so as not to change the spirit of the piece, to keep it homogeneous, in the way that painters do when the light is in harmony with their inspiration.

In the living room, Father stands by his easel and tries to capture the moods, the features of the day. He has many brushes and many colours and he paints the moment as he sees and feels it in his heart, without fabrication: the wind in the branches, the

scuds of snow, the fields made smaller by drifts, sagging line fences that have one strand of wire showing, the snow-smothered hay
ricks, the heavy swirls of a surly van Gogh sky. But he is from no
particular school or provincial night class whose academic teach-
ings can take the personality out of a picture. So his paintings have
an authenticity and can be identified at a glance. He is a true artist
right now and will be so again in the next snowfall or perhaps the
next great sunset. "True art don't come easy," he tells me.

In the old hawthorn tree by the kitchen door – where some
red berries cling, like the ones we paint with chalk on blackboards
at Christmastime – a moose-bird flits about, like the rustling of a
dead leaf, its small sad voice audible, the wind and snow ruffling its
feathers. These are the only things that are left to fight the season-
change, contrast the day's bleakness with hints of the past seasons.
It is in the wintertime that this inspired bird finds its lifelong partner, mates on the coldest of days, to nest with their young in a
blizzard. And I wonder if their togetherness, their trueness to each
other, has also been influenced by the tempest. They are the living
memories of rugged country people, long gone, they say.

Later in the day there are broken razor blades in the wind.
Tips of oat and corn-straw show through the snow. The weaker
reeds bend, the stronger ones stand, to make caves that glow red
with embroidered edges, a scattering of crystals, smooth and un-
tracked, as the eventual sun, the brighter Paul Gauguin sky, reflects
our window frames upon the kitchen floor. The road is ungraded
and there are two-foot cliffs at the back door. I shovel battlefield
trenches through beach sand that blocks our summer passages, the
snow blowing back in my face as if only it can tell me when the
magic is gone, and that I should wait until the assault is over.

And then the children come, crunching, crunching, on rub-
ber boots, leaving tracks that are being held together by vapour
trail-like patterns. They resemble the designs we make in our
games of fox and geese. It seems like the children appreciate any
kind of weather, and their voices are also musical and loud, especially on storm days. (I am too old to be one of them and too

young to be in town without a parent.) In the yard, they start a snowball, tiny at first, rolling, rolling, until it takes three of them to make it turn, gathering straw in its layers as it goes and on the ends that turn up in front of them, a jelly-roll-like mixture, with little sleeping insects in their winter layers, packed around with slush. With caked mittens, they roll another, and another not as big, and there is a series of grassy sidewalks leading up to a scarecrow that is out of season. With ashes from the parlour stove, they paint the eyes and smiling mouth, wrap an old plaid scarf around its neck, and place a beaver hat on its bald head. They dance in circles to celebrate their creation, a snowperson held together with straw.

But all too soon, seeing that it is already growing soft on the shallow side from exposure to the elements – or the straw that is in it – they start bombing the steamy snowperson with sticks and stones, the way people do each other, until it crumbles in the yard, topples to the ground like a Trojan horse, melts away, and is forgotten. It is just another childish outdoor game, waging assault on a person made of straw, to leave a scatter of ashes.

And I think, There is great inspiration, great insight in the first snowfall of the season.

The snowplow thunders past, blowing smoke into the hedge grove, to make a mountain range of fleece by the wire fence. Children run to the highway to watch the machine, with its bright lights, go by. But there are no runner tracks that loop near the barns as yet. No one is working a horse on this turbulent day. And I think there is something magical in a storm, something of a letdown when it's gone, the clearing. We grow dull and become our old common selves again, fearing we may fall forever into solitude, habit, even a deep sleep, the way that winter is.

WINTER ROAD

I WOULD NOT BE TELLING YOU THIS – FORTY YEARS later – had things not turned out the way they did: that two months after the Christmas of '75, my aunt Lillian died of a heart attack at her place in Houlton, Maine (the ashes brought home for burial), and that in her will she left me her Miramichi cottage, as well as a scholarship fund to get my degrees in music and literature at Mount Allison University. I now read short stories and play piano (Beethoven and Tchaikovsky) at school auditoriums and seniors' homes, especially at Christmastime, in the hopes that someone will get inspired as I did on a winter's night, the memories of which live inside me as I write this essay.

For the evening of December 23 that year, my mother had organized a sleigh ride. One of our neighbours had horses and a bobsled and was offering rides to the public. But this party was for my family and a few relations, along with Father Dolan, the Anglican priest from St. Peters, a Jack Falstaff-like man wearing snow boots and a long winter cassock. He strolled about our farmhouse, sipping scotch, while quoting Dylan Thomas, a writer none of us had read, though we masked our indifference.

It was all about Carol. She had arrived early that morning from Ottawa, having driven her BMW all night on snowy roads. And while she was home, Mother went out of her way to make things happen, as if my youngest sister was cut from a more refined cloth than I, and our worlds had to be lifted to a new dimension to please or appease her. It was like I was the steadfast spinster, true and blue to my folks, carrying the country load to keep it all going, until Carol came – dressed like a china doll – and then I was forgotten, until she went back to Ontario. And after three days at home, when she left, there was a lot of talk about how great she looked and how successful she had become. It happened every year.

Mum had planned this event, right down to the finest detail. She made arrangements for the teamster to bring his horses and sledge right up to our front door – all our outdoor lamps were lighted. After a few spirits, the family – Mum, Papa, sisters, brother, aunts and uncles, nieces and nephews – filed across the veranda, so entwined with dead ivy, the floor snapping and cracking from the frost, and took our seats on bales of hay in the long plank box. We covered ourselves with wraps and snuggled against one another, while the harness-studded strawberry roans, puffing steam, pranced back the snow-broken road, through fields of shortened corn stubble, projecting rosehip bushes, and frozen ponds that sparkled like stained glass, on towards the heavy woods.

The horses' shod hooves kicked up the icy, half-moon impressions, as taut reins kept the animals moving at a trot against the crunch and heave of the runners, while the teamster hollered, "Gee!" and "Haw!" to keep them true to one another. We passed windfall trees and sheaves of withered bracken, the half-frozen brook, a sunken stream of steeped tea. And from off the tree limbs there were little puffs of snow being scattered. It clung to our coats and caps and did not melt. Even in winter, nature has a beauty all of its own, I thought. Some of us turned up our collars and cradled our ears in gloved palms. As the traces strained, the harness jingled and the horses' bearded nostrils became white pincushions, the sleds bumping along as everyone sang, "Jingle bells, Jingle all the way."

Dressed in my wool mackinaw with a knitted toque pulled over my forehead, I sat on the back as the party followed old runner tracks that looped among white birches. And there was a hazy half-moon, sitting upon the treetops of a wintery sky, a storm

pending. How romantic, I thought. How nice it is to go to the
woods, knowing I do not have to get off at the end of the road
and work with an axe and saw. I can still hear the snoring of the
chainsaw as it ate its way through the bleeding fir trees. I rubbed
my ears with bare hands, as trees dropped snow that went inside
my coat collar. Some of this stuck to my shoulders to make my
coat steam. And after dark when we got home from work, I was
asked to carry the heavy buckets of water from the spring, bring
into the house the night's stove wood, because by that time of day
Papa was snow blind. Things have certainly changed for the better
since I was young, I thought. If only Carol could look close enough
to realize that good things can happen here at home, and the days
of winter poverty, cultural or materialistic, are a thing of the past.
It is just a matter of letting go of the ghost.

She must have seen that our houses were by then insulated,
and with concrete foundations – no longer did we bank the sills
with fir boughs in autumn – and that our floors were warm, and
everyone had running water and a bathroom. We had a big television, and in the dining room, I had a library of books from where
I got my high school education (GED) and was studying literature
by way of a correspondence course. We were driving good cars and
trucks, and I had bought an upright piano and ordered lessons,
How to Play in Ten Easy Steps, from Ray Hammerton of Winnipeg.

Times were not like they were before Carol went away, when
the family – girls included – went to the woods in the mornings, in
all weather, and worked until dark, especially in the weeks leading
up to Christmas. Every year, when Carol came home, thinking, I
suppose, that there was still hardship on our farm, she coaxed me
to go with her back to Ontario, where she would get me a job with
Canada Post. Good intentions. But I would not leave my home
province, or my aged parents who needed a homecare worker.
And also, I was getting my degree, writing those difficult memories
into essays.

Still, I looked at Carol with a jealous envy. I could not help
noticing how pretty she was, with the little fur-collared jacket and

the home-knit headband that was pulled down over her page-boy blonde hair, her nose pink-tipped from the cold. And her big blue eyes that flashed at this or that person. In the moonlight, I could see those eyes, even though I was sitting fifteen feet from her. I had never seen her more excited and happy. And I wondered if it was from the gin, or maybe she was just glad to be home, have a bit of fun among people who did not lay it on. Of course, she loved the attention, having picked up some of the Ontario pretentiousness, and confidence. (It was a thing I could never do.) She stood at the front of the sled, her back to the driver, and directed the music in the way that a conductor does with an orchestra. And the winter trees hung in crystals. Sometimes when a runner dropped into a rut and the box tilted sideways, Carol staggered and had to hang on to the teamster's coat to keep from falling overboard. At that point, laughter replaced the singing.

Two miles into the woods, when the driver turned the horses to follow the same runner tracks home, Carol changed the song to "Take Me Home, Country Road."

Back at the house, after everyone undid their scarves and coats, the guests helped themselves – potluck style – to more gin, whisky, and wines. Many of the men were beer-drinkers who had brought their own brew in cases. They sloshed it down straight from bottles, and rather than climb the stairs to the bathroom, went out the back door, stood on the step, and urinated into a snowbank, making steamy orange tunnels, and creating puffs of cold, gray vapour with each passage inside, and for the moment, filling the kitchen with a damp chill. The aura around this old country habit annoyed me, especially with Father Dolan and Carol being there. I thought, save for the genetic ties, this is not really the circle she wants to be with anymore. This might be a good party for us, but for her there is no meaningful conversation, no contrasting political views, no philosophic discussions on women's issues. The talk was all gossip and trivial. And she kept harping at me to lose weight, do something with my hair.

"Thank God, Father Dolan brings a bit of culture to help balance things," she said.

I thought, But these good country people will be here if I am in a jam and need them, more so than a government worker or even the priest, a so-called "Oxford man" who is also putting on airs. But I did not say anything. It was an argument we had had before. Of course, Carol knew that I had given up on cosmetics fifteen years before when Steven Grant was killed in a snowmobile accident, having kissed me goodnight and left our place to visit a cousin on the next farm. I had become a one-man woman at that time. And people told me – years later – they could see a touch of loneliness in my eyes. I mean, how do you deal with something like that?

Now we were being served chili beans and sauce with the homemade brown bread that Mum had made during the previous week. Everyone stood with an overflowing paper plate. My brother Johnny did not eat; instead he drank from a flask. He was pleased when Mum asked him to give us a tune. He stood in a corner of the kitchen and played hornpipes and reels to help keep the chivalry alive. And the screech of his fiddle in its high pitches made the windowpanes, the glass lamps, and the empty wine tumblers ring. Papa joked that not only did Johnny need practice, but lessons as well. Still, some of the men put down their plates, swung one another, and whooped. When the music ended, they clapped their hands, took another beer, and got into deer hunting.

Papa was a man who, even when he was young, looked old – like Gary Cooper in the movies. At this time, limping, he brought the Christmas tree in from the shed to stand in the parlour beside the piano. And I could smell the flavour of its balsam as the women and children joined Carol and me to decorate it. They were the same old decorations from my girlhood, the top star needing Scotch tape to keep it held together.

Through this, my aunt Lillian, a silver-haired woman in her eighties, sat by the fire in an elegant pose. A widow, she had been a schoolteacher in Houlton, Maine, for thirty years, but refused to become an American citizen. (She was well-to-do, her father having moved to the USA in the '30s to thrive in the potato business.) Each year she came home to her cottage for the summer and then Christmas. As the women, my mother among them, sipped their brandy and talked about the old days in Millerton – the school, the church, the skating parties on the river, the reflections of which were delightful – Johnny's sons, Wilson and Harry, took turns going to the front of the room and doing a school recitation. Through the fall, John had the boys rehearse the poetry for this reason and there was applause as Wilson stood near the piano and recited a verse by Longfellow, Aunt Lillian's favourite when she went to Bowdoin College.

> *Often I think of the beautiful town*
> *That is seated by the sea;*
> *Often in thought go up and down*
> *The pleasant streets of that dear old town,*
> *And my youth comes back to me.*

He finished the poem, took a bow, and returned to his seat.

There was applause from all hands, the men having come in from the kitchen to pay attention, in the way that grown-ups might listen to a fairy tale intended for children. And they laughed good-naturedly.

"That's such a wonderful piece. Will there ever be another poet as great as Longfellow?" Aunt Lillian said, wiping a tear. "We went to the same school, you know."

"Oh yes. I think so," I said.

"Yes, certainly there are many," Father Dolan said. "But without the period's telling metre and rhyme."

"I guess the poem speaks louder to me because it takes me back to my college days," Aunt Lillian said. She glanced at the dark December night outside the window.

Harry appeared nervous as he stood by the piano.

> *Whose woods these are I think I know*
> *His house is in the village though*
> *He will not see me stopping here*
> *To see his woods fill up with snow.*

He finished the poem, took a bow, and returned to *his* seat.

More applause, more chuckles from the men who then returned to the kitchen.

"It's so nice to listen to that poem when it is snowing out," Aunt Lillian said.

Everyone went to the window to see the snowflakes twisting and curling under the lamps.

I sat in a high-back wingchair by the fire and read a poem entitled "Winter." It was, in fact, one of Shakespeare's songs from the plays – *Love's Labour's Lost* – something I had learned from the literature courses. As I read, Harry crouched behind the chair where he could not be seen and did the sound effects to lines such as "Then nightly sings the staring owl, tu-whit, tu-who," and "Greasy Joan doth keel the pot."

From this skit there was laughter, especially when Harry got the signals wrong and tu-who'd when he should have stirred the pot.

To keep things moving, I sat at the piano and plunked with two fingers. Everyone – including the men from the kitchen – came around me to sing "White Christmas" and "Silver Bells." There was a great contrast of voices, some gruff, others shrill. A few started singing off-time and off-key and they ended singing off-time and off-key.

Then Mum asked Aunt Lillian if she would play the piano.

"Dorothy, do you have anything sheeted?" Lillian asked.

"Sheeted?"

"Yes, sheet music, you know. . . the notes on paper?"

"Oh yes . . . yes . . . no, Lillian. There's no such thing around here."

Lillian took a seat at the piano and began to play – from memory – a classical piece from her music-lessoned youth. Her face was uplifted as if she were reading the music from a mural on the ceiling, her slippers reaching for the pedals as though she were pumping an old-fashioned sewing machine. And no matter how many wrong notes she struck, she never let go of the piece's rhythm. Instead, she came down hard when she found the proper key, sometimes repeating a phrase to get it right.

I was fascinated by the voice of the piano, the delicate colours being played with such precision. They stirred feelings inside me never before experienced from live music. I fought back a tear. I had heard that piece before, perhaps on the radio, perhaps at a school recital, but it remained invisible until I listened to it being performed here at home, on my own piano and by a relative, so that it was – to me – its first rendition, a thing that I was ashamed to admit, and something I would never forget.

"What's the name of that beautiful piece?" I asked.

"It's Beethoven's *Moonlight Sonata in C Sharp Minor*. I can no longer do justice to it because of my arthritic fingers. I would not even attempt to play the Thirteenth or Fourteenth Quarter as I did years ago at the Conservatory."

"It sounded like perfection to me," I said. "I never heard music so moving. Like Wordsworth, Beethoven paints a beautiful picture. He brings back the atmosphere of a more romantic age."

"Romance can be a dangerous escape," Carol put in.

"I'll chance it for a while," I said.

"For me it brings back the age of practise, practise, practise," Aunt Lillian said. "I no longer hear the piece for what it actually stands for; instead it inspires symbols from my school days. That's what happens when you study music – everyone else appreciates it more, and reads it for what it's meant to say, but for the musician, well, . . . it's work."

"There's such nobility in the arts, such dedication needed to express those accomplished little brush strokes," I said. "This night, I swear, is a new starting point for me."

Aunt Lillian got up from the piano to sit in her chair by the fire. She sat with her back straight, hands folded on her lap, her legs crossed at the ankles as if she were posing for a portrait.

"I suppose there's nothing wrong with someone starting into music at your age," she said, facing me. "But it takes many years to accomplish the classics."

. For a moment I was saddened by the fact that I had grown up without having a music lesson, and was now oblivious to what much of it stood for. But one would have to know the circumstances of that day – that Johnny and I had quit elementary school to help keep the farm going – to understand my predicament, as some of these people would not, especially Father Dolan, or even Carol, who was ten years younger, had not worked hard, and had gone to university. The times had gotten better for her generation. There was just no place for classical music in my girlhood.

"Of course, we cannot live solely in the arts as some egocentrics do, who know more about music and literature than they do about life itself," Aunt Lillian said. "The arts have their places but in most cases they are only intonations of real life. Minnie, I don't know why I am telling *you* this. I know you have experienced life in the roughest form growing up here. But I believe that to be a virtue and not a liability as you seem to think. Those are the conditions from out of which our best characters are conceived."

"Hear! Hear!" Papa said as if he were waking from a dead sleep. He clapped his hands, twice. "Minnie, Johnny, Carol, fetch me another drink of that good wine Lillie brought."

"Of course, diversity is important." Lillian turned to face Carol. "My husband, who was a mechanical engineer, could not find the middle C on a piano. So there was no chance one of us would be influenced by the other. We left each other free to pursue our own separate worlds. Like your sister, he had a heart of gold, yet was so provincial in his manner. People loved him for the sincerity of his affection, his selflessness. I went to things with him and he came to things with me. He was always confident in social circles. We supported each other. If you love someone you want to see them achieve their goal. Otherwise, it is all a deception and no one can pretend forever." She turned to face me. "So, Minnie, don't be ashamed of your background, be you a farmer, milkmaid, or a shopkeeper. A caretaker is as important as a teller of stories or an essayist. We have to do what we love best, that is the important thing. A dream is from the heart, and without following it we cannot find true happiness. But to pursue one's dream, however romantic, is a hard old road and we need support and love while we are attempting it."

"That's my point, Lillian," Carol said. Her eyes were popping. "The real thing, here and now, is what's important, not a romantic whim, not a piece of music from long ago. We cannot live in a world of nostalgia."

"Carol takes everything I say literally," I said. "The real thing is love and support whatever road we decide to go as we follow our hearts. Good music brings pleasure. It's an escape. For the elderly, nostalgia is not a dirty word."

"I think Minnie deserves a lot of credit for trying to achieve these things at her age," Mum said. "She has been into the books every evening, and then working the piano. A family has to get behind the one who tries to reach higher."

"Thank you, Mama!" I said.

"The classes of the intellect, especially when it comes to the arts, take no account of one's birthplace, genetics, or age, especially a soul person like Minnie. In fact, I think the rugged experiences of her past, her hurts and disappointments – because she is so sensitive – are a great asset. You have to have suffered pain before you can write about it," Lillian said. She appeared to be annoyed with Carol.

"And, Minnie, it has nothing to do with the big school," Aunt Lillian went on. "When it came to culture, I got less out of Bowdoin College than I did the Millerton high school. For in the end we have to self-educate as you are trying to do. In your case, wanting to write, to recapture the hardship of your girlhood, you are unique in your genuineness, your individuality, your style. And all things being equal, the inimitable voice is the better art form. I was a mature student when I went to college, having spent ten years in a sanatorium. We are never too old to pursue our dreams."

I felt that the evening was the most wonderful of my life. Everything I had been secretly dreaming and praying for since Steven died had come together. I was so happy I got up from my chair and skipped through the house, hugging first Papa and Mum, then the dog, then the boys and girls, and finally Johnny and Carol. I wanted to make a speech, give a toast, reveal to those people the hard road I had come, the internal struggles I had encountered, and the path I would continue on until I had made a success of things. But I thought better of it – why embarrass myself and my family with a sad tale here?

"Minnie, you have had too much to drink, again!" Carol snapped.

"No, no. I'm not drunk, I am just happy. Is there anything wrong with my being happy for once?"

"No, no. Be happy! Please, be happy," Carol pleaded.

"Could I get you more brandy, Aunt Lillian?" I asked.

"No, thank you, Minnie. I have had enough." She yawned and, covering her mouth with a hand, apologized for her tiredness. "Is it still storming out?"

"Yes, it's snowing. I'll walk with you to your cottage."

I wrapped a long scarf around the collar of my coat and put on my stocking-leg cap. After hugs all around, Aunt Lillian and I walked into the snowy night, arm and arm, under the big oak trees that had a few remaining leaves that rattled – the piano music still playing inside us – on down that trackless winter road to her cottage where we embraced and said goodnight.

ACKNOWLEDGEMENTS

The story "Winter Road" was published in the *Telegraph-Journal* on December 24, 2016.

I would like to thank my first readers, Cynthia Lozier, Carol Nesbit, David Adams Richards, and Heather Browne, and Julia Swan for her editing work.

I would also like to thank Dennis Duffy from Trabon Group in Kansas City for his design of leaflets and his positive contributions.

BIOGRAPHY

Wayne Curtis was born in Keenan, New Brunswick, in 1943. He was educated at the local schoolhouse and St. Thomas University, where he majored in English. He started writing prose when he was in grade school. His work has been described by *Books in Canada* as "A pleasure to read, for no detail escapes his discerning eye." He has won the Richards Award for short fiction as well as the CBC Drama Award and in 2019 the Lieutenant-Governor's Award for High Achievement in the English Literary Arts. He has received grants from the New Brunswick Arts Board (artsnb) and The Canada Council. He has been a contributor to several newspapers including the *National Post* and *The Globe and Mail* as well as commercial magazines: *The Reader's Digest, Quill & Quire, Outdoor Canada, The Fly Fisherman (USA), Atlantic Insight,* and *The Atlantic Advocate*. Wayne's stories have appeared in the literary journals *The Cormorant, Pottersfield Portfolio, Nashwaak Review, Antigonish Review, New Brunswick Reader,* and *New Maritimes* and the anthologies *Atlantica, Country Roads, The STU Reader, Winter House The Christmas Secret,* and *Winter*. His short stories have been dramatized on CBC radio and CBC television.

In the spring of 2005, Wayne Curtis received an Honorary Doctorate Degree (Letters) from St. Thomas University. In 2014, he was awarded the Order of New Brunswick. In 2018, he was awarded the Canadian Senate Sesquicentennial Medal.

Wayne has lived in southern Ontario, Yukon Territories, and Cuba. He currently divides his time between the Miramichi River and the City of Fredericton, New Brunswick.

BOOKS BY WAYNE CURTIS

Winter Road (2020)

Fishing the High Country (2018)

Homecoming (2017)

In the Country (2016)

Sleigh Tracks in New Snow (2014)

Of Earthly and River Things (2012)

Long Ago and Far Away (2010)

Night Train to Havana (2008)

Wild Apples (2006)

Green Lightning (2005)

Monkeys in a Looking Glass (2005)

Fly Fishing the Miramichi (2003)

River Stories (2000)

Last Stand (1999)

Preferred Lies (1998)

River Guides of the Miramichi (1997)

Fishing the Miramichi (1994)

One Indian Summer (1993)

Currents in the Stream (1988)